"I don't know why she's doing this, but Darcy would never hurt those kids."

"She already has," Peter snapped. "She kidnapped them. Don't you remember how that felt?"

He sighed, not wanting to tell Alanna about his own past, but wondering if that was the best way to reach her.

"I do remember. I still have nightmares about it sometimes. I know you don't understand how I can—" she took an audible breath "—love them."

"I do understand that." Or at least, he understood that she thought what she felt was love, instead of a complicated mix of fear and dependency multiplied over fourteen years. "Stockholm syndrome is real. It's—"

Her snort of disbelief cut him off. She looked offended. "I got a psychology degree after I left Alaska. I understand why you think that's what's happening here, but don't forget—I'm the one who turned them in. They both went to jail because I left that note. My... Julian died because of me."

Acknowledgments

Writing a book is often just me, my parrot and my computer. But the process of bringing a book to life takes many! My deepest thanks to my editor, Denise Zaza; my agent, Kevan Lyon; and everyone behind the scenes at Harlequin who helped get *Alaska Mountain Rescue* to readers. A special thanks to my family and friends, who are always my biggest cheerleaders: Andrew Gulli, Chris Heiter, Kathryn Merhar, Alan Merhar, Caroline Heiter, Kristen Kobet and Robbie Terman. And a special thanks to my writer pals, who met me virtually or in person to get all the words: Heather Novak, Dana Nussio, Tyler Anne Snell and Janie Crouch.

ALASKA MOUNTAIN RESCUE

Elizabeth Heiter

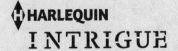
HARLEQUIN
INTRIGUE

This book is for my new brother and sister, Farris and Lamia,
who have made the word *in-law* sound amazing.

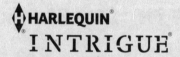

ISBN-13: 978-1-335-40151-9

Recycling programs
for this product may
not exist in your area.

Alaska Mountain Rescue

Copyright © 2020 by Elizabeth Heiter

This edition published by arrangement with Harlequin Books S.A.

For questions and comments about the quality of this book,
please contact us at CustomerService@Harlequin.com.

Harlequin Enterprises ULC
22 Adelaide St. West, 40th Floor
Toronto, Ontario M5H 4E3, Canada
www.Harlequin.com

Printed in U.S.A.

Elizabeth Heiter likes her suspense to feature strong heroines, chilling villains, psychological twists and a little romance. Her research has taken her into the minds of serial killers, through murder investigations and onto the FBI Academy's shooting range. Elizabeth graduated from the University of Michigan with a degree in English literature. She's a member of International Thriller Writers and Romance Writers of America. Visit Elizabeth at www.elizabethheiter.com.

Books by Elizabeth Heiter

Harlequin Intrigue

K-9 Defense
Secret Investigation
Alaska Mountain Rescue

The Lawmen: Bullets and Brawn

Bodyguard with a Badge
Police Protector
Secret Agent Surrender

The Lawmen

Disarming Detective
Seduced by the Sniper
SWAT Secret Admirer

Visit the Author Profile page at Harlequin.com.

CAST OF CHARACTERS

Alanna Morgan—She spent most of her childhood with people who kidnapped her. When she turned them in, she thought she'd never return to Alaska. But when the woman who pretended to be her mother escapes from jail—and grabs more kids—Alanna thinks it's her duty to help. Still, she's not prepared for the memories—or the temptation of Peter Robak.

Peter Robak—The rookie police officer thinks Alanna can help him prove himself by leading him to the kidnapper. But as he falls for her, he may have to make a choice: Alanna's life or the children.

Chance—Alanna's loyal St. Bernard was a therapy dog back in Chicago, but in Alaska, he discovers a natural talent for snow rescue.

Darcy Altier—She and her husband raised Alanna with love. But since her "daughter" turned them in, no one knows whether Alanna's presence will help bring Darcy in peacefully—or make her more dangerous.

Tate Emory—Peter's partner in the Desparre PD reluctantly follows Peter's lead, hoping that using Alanna as bait will bring Darcy out of hiding.

Keara Hernandez—The Desparre PD chief thinks Alanna is a liability—one that may cost Peter his career.

Chapter One

The whispers started the moment she stepped into town.

"It's *her*. The kidnapped girl. The one from five years ago."

"The one who almost got her real sister killed?"

Alanna tried to ignore the sidelong glances from the two women peering at her from the open door of the grocery store. In a place like Desparre, Alaska, the stares and chatter were likely to bring more people.

Alanna hunched her shoulders, trying to disappear into her heavy coat as she picked up her pace. Still, she felt their accusatory gazes bore into her. The pace of her breathing picked up, sweat breaking out all over her body. This was the side effect of sending the "parents" who'd raised her for fourteen years to jail and then returning to another state, to a family she'd tried so hard to remember but didn't quite fit into anymore. The side effect of spending too long dodging reporters desperate to be the one to break her silence and get the inside story of her abduction.

The voices faded as the women disappeared back into the grocery store, one of a handful of buildings that lined Desparre's small downtown area. It looked so tiny compared to the suburb on the outskirts of Chicago where she'd returned after living in the remote wilderness of Alaska with the family who'd kidnapped her.

Even after being gone for five long years, in many ways, Alaska still felt like home.

Alanna took a deep breath of the crisp, cool air and closed her eyes, letting the familiar sounds and smells and sights calm her. At her side, her St. Bernard, Chance, recognized her method for coping with anxiety and scooted up against her, then promptly sat.

A minute later, the sound of Chance's low, sustained growl made her eyes pop back open.

The St. Bernard was definitely a gentle giant, more likely to thump his tail and wait for a belly rub than go after anyone. But his size and his warning growl never failed to make people who were a little too aggressive back up fast.

In the past, Chance had used that growl on a handful of particularly determined reporters who'd stuck with her for years, following her around and ambushing her at the most unexpected times, seeking a candid photo or a sound bite. Because no matter how much time passed, she was still one of *those* women. A name that had made national headlines. A story she could never outgrow. Today, Chance was using his growl on the police officer who'd somehow managed to get close while her eyes were shut.

His startling blue eyes darted to her dog, then back to her. "Miss, do you need hel—"

The words trailed off as those blue eyes widened

slightly. In a face made up of sharp angles and pale skin, his eyes were especially compelling. His tone was less friendly, more suspicious as he said, "Alanna Altier?"

"Morgan," she corrected. The name of her birth family, instead of the family who'd raised her for most of her childhood. After five years, the name Morgan was finally starting to feel less foreign on her lips.

"Morgan," he repeated. His gaze swept the space behind her, as if the woman who'd raised her—who'd helped kidnap her and four other children over the span of eighteen years and then escaped from police custody five days ago—would suddenly appear.

Anxiety started to swell again and Chance scooted even closer, his warm fur pressing against her leg, his big head nuzzling her.

Absently petting him, Alanna kept her eyes on the officer. She didn't recognize him. Not that she would—the Altiers had kept her and her "siblings" far from prying eyes, especially law enforcement eyes. She'd been to town before, but more often she'd stayed home, spending most of her days inside the house she'd helped build. Or in the dozen acres surrounding it that the Altiers owned, a buffer from them and the rest of the world. At times, it had felt like an oasis. At others, it had seemed more like a cage.

The officer's narrowed eyes locked on hers again, unsettling in their singular focus. "I thought you'd moved back to Chicago, with your real family."

It was somewhere between a statement and a question and Alanna tried not to fixate on the word *real*. She loved the Morgans, the parents who'd enveloped her in hugs the moment she'd stepped back through their door, who'd kept all her belongings from when she had disappeared from their lives at five years old. The big brother, who'd stared at her with huge, teary eyes before breaking into a shaky smile and whispering, "I can't believe it. You're finally home." The older sister, who'd traveled across the country on the slimmest of leads, who'd almost died trying to save her.

"I did," Alanna finally answered. "But—"

"But Darcy Altier is back to her old tricks. And you think…what? She's coming back here?"

Darcy Altier. The woman she'd called "Mom" for fourteen years. Alanna had always known she'd been kidnapped, remembered with startling clarity the moment when Julian Altier had yanked her out of her yard in Illinois and into his car. But Darcy and Julian had never harmed her. They'd treated her like their own child, held her when she cried, smiled with her in happy times. They'd loved her. Despite everything else, she knew that.

Over those fourteen years, she'd grown to love them, too. She'd also grown to love the other children the Altiers had kidnapped, her "siblings." She missed all of them with an ache that was hard to explain to anyone, least of all the family who'd waited and searched for her all those years.

"Well?" the officer pressed, shifting so his right side was angled toward her. The side where a gun was holstered at his hip.

Her anxiety ratcheted up again and Chance stood up, stepping slightly forward. Protecting her, the way he'd done since the moment she'd brought him home. He'd been a tiny, emaciated puppy then, who had somehow managed to survive in cruel conditions until he was taken away and eventually ended up in her care. Now, though small for a St. Bernard, he outweighed her by twenty pounds.

Alanna put her hand on his back, pressed down slightly. Telling him to stay put.

"I don't know," Alanna answered, her gaze darting to the police station behind him. She *was* here for Darcy, because from the instant she'd seen the news report about her "mother's" escape, she'd known it deep down. Nowhere had felt like home to any of them the way Alaska had. But she wasn't about to say that to an officer who'd stared at her with barely veiled suspicion since the moment he'd realized who she was.

Seeming to recognize her discomfort, the officer took a step backward. But he still held the odd angle and she couldn't stop staring at that weapon.

"I think we got off on the wrong foot," he said, the words sounding strangled. "I'm Peter Robak."

Robak. The name floated around in her mind, vaguely familiar, and Alanna tried to place it. Before she could, he was speaking again.

"Why are you back in Desparre, Alanna?"

"I…" She was on a fool's quest. One that would have horrified her family back in Chicago if she'd told them about it in person, instead of in the note she had left. One that had definitely frustrated her boss, when she'd called to let him know she was taking time off in the middle of the work week and wasn't sure when she'd be back.

But who else knew Darcy Altier like she did? It was one thing that Darcy had escaped police custody. Alanna knew the woman belonged in jail, but that didn't mean she liked the idea of the person who'd helped raise her being behind bars. If it had simply been an escape, Alanna would have stayed in Chicago. But when a child had gone missing...

Straightening her shoulders, Alanna told him, "I was actually on my way to the police station."

Peter eyed her with distrust for another minute, then stepped slightly aside. He swept his hand forward, gesturing for her to lead the way.

She felt him close behind her for every step of the short walk into the police station. Opening the door, she led Chance inside with her, not caring how the officers would feel about that. Technically, he was a service dog.

Inside the station, a wall of warm air hit her, reminding Alanna of just how cold it was outside. In her years living here, she'd gotten used to it and when she'd made the trip back, she'd packed appropriately. Yanking the hat off her head and unwinding her scarf, she looked around.

It was a tiny station, with a counter up front and an officer who glanced up, then returned to his paperwork when he saw Peter.

Peter said, "Alanna Alt...Morgan is here. Is the Chief around?" And suddenly the officer looked a lot more interested.

"Hang on a sec," he replied, giving her one last

look before he disappeared behind a door marked Police Only.

Alanna planted her feet in a wider stance, tipping her chin up. A trick she'd taught herself to help her feel more confident, more in control. Chance's familiar form pressing against her leg didn't hurt, either.

From a back room, the police chief appeared, leaving the door to the bullpen open behind her. She was young for her position, but strode through the door with a genuine confidence Alanna envied. With the chief's dark hair pulled back into a bun and her expression somehow serious and friendly at the same time, Alanna could see her both putting victims at ease and scaring criminals.

The chief nodded once at Peter, then held out a hand. "How can I help you, Alanna?"

The officer who'd been sitting behind the counter settled back in his seat, this time ignoring his paperwork, unabashedly interested. Another officer stared at them through the open doorway, curiosity on his face. Alanna tried to shut them all out and just focus on the chief. Focus on the reason she'd come all this way, back to a place she thought she'd never see again.

"I…" Clearing her throat, Alanna said, "I'm sure you are already aware that Darcy Altier escaped from custody when she was allowed to go to my fa… Julian Altier's funeral. And that a child went missing a few miles from where she escaped and she's a suspect in the case."

It was a bold, dangerous move, something Alanna had never felt Darcy was capable of. At least, not until the moment Darcy had picked up a shotgun and fired at Alanna's sister, Kensie, who'd flown to Alaska to try to save her.

Shutting that memory out, Alanna continued, "I think she might come back to Desparre. I want to help you find Darcy." She wanted to help them bring her in safely.

The chief smiled, the expression half pitying and half amused, and Alanna felt her cheeks flush deep red.

The woman reached out and put a hand on Alanna's upper arm. She squeezed gently, as if Alanna was the sheltered, scared nineteen-year-old from five years ago. Back then, officers from a neighboring town had taken her away from the only family she'd known for fourteen years and brought her to the hospital, where her biological sister waited.

Now Alanna was twenty-four, in the process of getting her master's degree and catching up on all the things she hadn't really known she'd missed while she was hidden away in Alaska. But she suddenly felt nineteen again when the chief said, "We appreciate that, but I think we've got it handled."

The chief continued with words of sympathy about the man who'd kidnapped her, who'd been a father to her for so many years. The man who'd been buried five days ago, whose service Alanna had longed to attend, but hadn't, knowing how it would hurt the family who'd missed her since she was five.

Alanna barely heard the words. Instead, she heard the snicker from the officer behind the counter.

Humiliated, Alanna spun back in the direction she'd entered.

The officer who'd brought her into the station—Peter Robak, who she remembered suddenly as someone she'd seen on TV a few years ago, a war reporter who'd almost died covering a hostage release—stood in her way.

He stepped slightly aside as she pushed past him, back into the frigid Alaskan air with Chance at her side, like always. She hurried across the unpaved street toward the truck she'd rented when her plane set down at the closest airport, which was still hours away. Then she stopped, spun back around, and looked up and down the small street. Despite the fact that it was still only midday, it was empty now.

Her St. Bernard stared up at her with his soft brown eyes. Then his head pivoted at the sound of a hawk's call overhead. Chance wasn't used to the vast emptiness of Desparre compared to the suburb outside busy Chicago where they lived.

Right now, there was only a light sprinkling of snow on the Desparre streets. But that could change at any time. Winter came here early, hard and fast. Sometimes, it got hit with enough snow to make leaving Desparre impossible until spring came.

When Chance's gaze returned to hers, there was a question there, as if he was asking, *What are we doing here?*

Being in the police station had made coming back here feel like a big mistake. But somewhere nearby, Darcy and a small child were hiding. Alanna was sure of it. And that child—like some of the "siblings" she'd grown up with—was young enough not to remember his family if they didn't find him in time.

For fourteen years, Alanna had been afraid to speak up, afraid to try to get help. At first, that fear had been because she hadn't known how her abductors would respond. Would they hurt her? Would they kill her? Later, it had been because, despite everything, she loved the Altiers and the four kids she'd called brothers and sisters. She'd become afraid of what would happen to all of them if she tried to sneak away and told anyone the truth.

For the past five years, she'd felt guilty about all of it. Seeing the pain she'd caused her biological parents and siblings Kensie and Flynn, wondering if some of the other kids wouldn't have been kidnapped if she'd spoken up sooner.

She couldn't change the past. But she could change the future.

This time, she wasn't staying silent. She wasn't going home and she wasn't staying out of this investigation, whether the police wanted her help or not.

"We're going to do this," she told Chance. "We're going to find them."

"SHE'S GOT A lot of nerve, showing up here," Peter muttered to no one in particular.

As usual, his partner, Tate Emory, heard him. "I don't know. I feel bad for her. Imagine what she's been through. It can't have been easy to write that note and turn in the only family she'd known since she was five years old."

Peter shifted and scowled at his partner, who'd strode over to stand beside him, moving silently. Or maybe

Peter just hadn't heard him, since Tate had come up on Peter's left side. The side where his hearing was mostly gone.

Being new to the force, new to policing in general, hadn't been a smooth transition for Peter. Most of the officers here still stared at him like the rookie he was. Worse, he knew plenty of them hadn't wanted him accepted onto the force in the first place because of his hearing disability. Some of them were still trying to push him out.

He'd never felt that from Tate. His partner had only been on the force for five years, just long enough to have been present for Alanna's dramatic rescue.

It had all started with a simple note, left between some money at a general store on the outskirts of Desparre. The note had been as straightforward as it was confusing, since at the time there'd been no indication Alanna was even alive, let alone that her kidnappers had taken other children. *My name is Alanna Morgan, from Chicago. I'm still alive. I'm not the only one.*

The FBI had done a quick investigation and called the note a hoax, yet another dead end in a more than decade-old cold case. But Alanna's sister had believed it, had traveled over three thousand five hundred miles across the country in search of a sister she'd only known for five short years. The rescue had been sensational, making national news and putting the sleepy town of Desparre in a spotlight it desperately wanted to avoid. Now that spotlight might be returning.

Back then, Peter had been overseas, doing something he thought he'd stick with until it was time to retire.

The scandal of the kidnapping had caught his attention only because he grew up in Luna, the little town next to Desparre where Alanna had finally been reunited with the sister who'd come to Alaska to find her.

Peter stared at the closed door Alanna had disappeared through, trying not to picture the embarrassment in her eyes. Yeah, he felt sorry for what she'd gone through, but five years had passed. Enough time to create a new life for herself with her real family, people who must have gone through hell thinking she was lost to them forever. She should have been home with them now, not out looking for a kidnapper. Because no matter what she said, he didn't quite believe she was here to put Darcy Altier back behind bars.

Alanna Morgan might have started out as a victim, but now she could choose her path in life. And every nuance in her voice, the flickers of emotion he'd seen in her eyes, told him she was choosing all wrong. She was here for Darcy Altier, all right, but not to get her arrested. To help her hide.

"Why do you think she believes Darcy returned to Desparre?" Tate asked.

Peter shrugged, his gaze still fixed on that closed door. It was a good question. Darcy Altier had been granted furlough to bury her husband, who'd been killed in jail. She'd managed to slip free of her guards and run, but that had been in Oregon, back near the prison. A smart woman would head as far from the site of her original crimes as possible. So why did Alanna think that Darcy was here? Why was *Alanna* here?

"They've been in contact." Peter spoke his thoughts out loud. It was the only logical explanation.

"Seriously?" Tate scoffed. "Alanna's the one who turned her in. You really think Darcy would reach out to her after that?"

Peter turned to look at his partner. Tate was a couple of inches taller than Peter's five-foot-ten-inch frame, his skin and hair a couple of shades darker. From the moment they'd met, Peter had felt a strange kinship with Tate, a sense that both of them had known hardship they didn't speak of, that both of them had a restless desire to move past it.

"This woman raised her since she was five years old," Peter insisted. "Alanna spent most of her childhood with her. I bet she barely remembered her real family. How much do *you* remember from before you were five?"

Tate shrugged. "Enough. Obviously Alanna remembered them or she wouldn't have left a note for them to find her."

"Sure, but then she continued to hide with the people who kidnapped her."

"That's a little harsh. She was nineteen. How much freedom do you think they gave her? You, of all people, should understand—"

Peter let out a humorless laugh. "Understand what? The lengths people will go to in order to protect someone who hurt them?"

That was something he definitely understood. He'd gotten an up-close look at the unnatural attachment a hostage could develop for their captor. That experience had destroyed his career as a war reporter—had destroyed much of the hearing in his left ear, too. There was no chance of recovering his hearing, no surgery or hearing aid that could improve it.

Peter had no doubt that Alanna had a similar unhealthy attachment, that she was suffering from serious delusions about the woman who'd stolen her away from her family. It made her motives questionable. Worse, it made her dangerous.

Tate was shaking his head, but Peter kept going. "You're right. I do understand. Ultimately, it doesn't matter if Alanna has spoken to Darcy or she just knows her well enough to predict her movements. If Darcy is crazy enough to actually come back here, Alanna is the key."

Speaking the words aloud made anticipation swell in his chest and his gaze dart back to the closed door. Alanna *was* the key—and not just to locating a fugitive and solving a kidnapping, but to Desparre's reputation as a quiet, safe place to be left alone. And to Peter's future on the Desparre police force.

"Uh-oh," Tate said. "I know *that* look."

"Alanna is going to lead us to Darcy Altier and the missing kid." He headed for the door, gesturing for his partner to follow. "We're not letting Alanna out of our sight until she does."

Chapter Two

Alanna stared through dense woods at the house where she'd grown up. She'd helped build it on this mountaintop, dragging wood alongside her "siblings" and helping her "parents" lift the framework into place. All those months of hard labor, of watching the house slowly take shape. When it was finally finished, she'd been proud of her home.

Now it looked derelict and empty, snow covering the driveway that no one had bothered to shovel. Likely no one wanted to buy a house built by a pair of kidnappers, once home to five stolen kids.

Once upon a time, she'd stared at it with happiness and love. Now, there was bitterness, too, with the memory of her "mother" and "older brother" firing weapons at Kensie as she risked her life to bring Alanna home.

Alanna swallowed hard as she stepped out of the truck she'd parked at the end of the gravel driveway. Chance bounded out after her, quick despite his size, loving the heavy snowfall in Alaska. He stuck close to her, a faithful companion who needed no leash.

She'd come here straight from the police station, not

even bothering to check in to her hotel yet. Now, she wondered if she should have taken a break, given herself a chance to emotionally acclimate to being back here.

Her attention snagged on broken bits of scattered wood. The sign with her "family's" name and a No Trespassing warning had been smashed to pieces.

She bent down and picked up the largest piece, a splintered slab of wood that read Altier. She ran her gloved fingertips over the hand-carved lettering, remembering when Darcy had made it. The urge to take it with her was strong, but what if her family in Chicago saw it? They'd be hurt and full of questions she didn't know how to answer any better now than she had five years ago, despite the degree in psychology she'd earned since coming home. So, instead, she set it carefully back on the snow, tucked her hands in her pockets and strode toward the house. Chance walked beside her, comfortable in the frigid weather that made Chicago seem mild.

It would be foolish for Darcy to come here. But she and Julian had spent so many years running from state to state, never staying long in one place, afraid to draw any attention. In this remote patch of Alaskan wilderness, they'd finally felt like they weren't being chased. They'd been willing to put down roots, trusted that the children they'd raised wouldn't turn them in for kidnapping them from families they either barely remembered or, in the case of Alanna's youngest "siblings," didn't remember at all.

Walking around the edge of the house, her feet sank into deeper snow that dampened her pants just below

Elizabeth Heiter

the knees, where her boots ended. She peered through each of the windows on the ground floor. Nothing. No sign that anyone was inside, no sign that anyone had been here in a long time.

The furniture they'd picked out or built had been moved around—chairs knocked over, drawers hanging open with the contents spilled. All the things she and her "family" had left behind, had never been able to come back to claim. Alanna rubbed the bare finger where she used to wear a worn ruby ring, an Altier family heirloom that was the only thing she'd taken with her back to Chicago. She'd stopped wearing it when she'd noticed her parents and siblings constantly eyeing it, though they'd never actually come out and asked what it meant to her.

Focusing on the house again, Alanna leaned closer, peering through the windows into the living room, looking for any sign that Darcy had been here recently. The dirt on the wooden floors had faded to a light gray with no new tracks in the dust. It was clearly old, from when a slew of police officers had traipsed through, looking for her "family" five years ago. Back then, they'd already fled, but not far enough, not fast enough. The police had caught up to them.

Alanna squeezed her eyes closed against the memory of a circle of officers training weapons on her "parents" and screaming at them to get down. Of watching Julian and Darcy be flattened to the ground in deep snow, officers' knees pressing hard into their backs as they were cuffed. Of her youngest "siblings" crying and clinging to her. Of her older "brother" scowling, the tension in his body telling her he might do something stupid.

Chance nudged his big head against her thigh, hard enough to almost make her stumble. Her eyes opened, a laugh breaking free despite the pain in her heart. "I know, boy. You don't understand what we're doing here." She sighed, stroking her gloved hand over his soft head. "I used to live here." Her attention drifted to the dense woods behind the house, the steep slope of a mountain that dropped off suddenly. Protection from fears she hadn't totally understood as a child. "I used to be happy here."

The rumble of an engine nearby made Chance's head swivel. Alanna peered around the edge of the house, toward the street. This part of Desparre wasn't on many maps. Houses were set apart by miles, far from the road and hard to find if you didn't know where you were going. They were up higher in the mountains, in an area more prone to avalanches and deeper snow. Even locals didn't often come this way without a reason.

Her heart rate picked up as she squinted at the street for any sign of life beyond the thick trees. Could it be Darcy? If it was, how would she react to Alanna's presence?

Five years ago, Alanna's older "brother" Johnny had started talking about wanting to get married. It had put an ache in Alanna's heart with the realization that she'd never have any memories with the family she'd tried for fourteen years to remember. Not unless she acted.

So, she had. When Julian had taken her into some stores on the outskirts of town, she'd slipped a note into the stack of bills they'd used to pay. She'd been so afraid Julian would notice. She hadn't been afraid he'd hurt her—she'd stopped fearing that long ago. But she *had* been scared of how he'd react if he found it.

Yes, he'd kidnapped her. There was no way to spin that; it was just wrong. But he'd loved her. He and Darcy had raised her; they'd homeschooled her in every subject so well that when she'd returned and taken her GED, it had been ridiculously easy. She'd sailed through college, too. But it hadn't just been academics. They'd taught her to be self-reliant in the dangerous wilderness, taught her skills that Kensie and Flynn still shook their heads at with awe. They'd raised her with love and, as the years went by, she couldn't stop herself from loving them, too.

Back then, she had been so focused on seeing her birth family again. She hadn't let herself consider the possible consequences for the people who'd raised her, or for the kids she'd called brothers and sisters, who she still missed desperately. She knew if she'd paused to think about all of that, she never would have done it.

The sound of the vehicle reached her ears again, this time the slow grind of tires over snow that hadn't been packed down yet. Was it Darcy, noticing the unfamiliar truck in the driveway, afraid to approach?

Alanna stepped out from behind the house, hurrying toward the street with Chance bounding after her. He loved the snow, thought it was a game, but she was too anxious to pay much attention. Would Darcy stop if she saw Alanna now? Or would she speed away?

When Alanna reached the street, a dark SUV backed quickly out of view. It was too quickly to decipher who was in the vehicle, but there were two people in the front seat. One thing Alanna knew for sure: it wasn't a child in the passenger seat. It looked like there were two men in the car.

Pinpricks of awareness swept across her arms. The Altiers had built this home in as secluded a spot as they could find. But that seclusion worked both ways. Right now, it meant no one would hear her cry for help.

Back in Chicago, the news stories had called her a hero, had highlighted how it all ended, with her leaving a note for her family to find her. But in Alaska, it was different. In Desparre, she wasn't the girl who'd helped five kids go home to families who missed them. She was the girl who'd put their sleepy, intentionally below-the-radar town on a national stage. She was the girl who'd been hiding in the woods for years, never reaching out for help. Because while the locals might have a live-and-let-live attitude about someone else's business, they also protected their own. If she'd asked, they'd all said, they would have helped her.

In all the years she'd lived in Desparre, she'd never asked. It was pretty clear some of them hated her for it.

"Chance, come on." She tapped her thigh twice, then ran for her truck, the dog close on her heels.

They hopped into the vehicle and then Alanna was speeding in the other direction, away from the strange SUV, away from the downtown. Deeper into the mountains.

"WE SCARED HER off." Tate stated the obvious as Alanna and her St. Bernard jumped into their truck and took off at a speed that would normally get them pulled over.

Silently, Peter cursed himself for getting too anxious, getting too close. But he'd been intrigued by the house deep in the wilderness where five kids had been hidden away for years. Like a lot of Alaska, Desparre was known for being a place where people could get lost. Most people were here for legitimate reasons—wanting to run from some tragedy in their life, wanting to recharge in Alaska's wild beauty or even wanting to hide from someone who meant them harm. But Alaska sometimes attracted people for the wrong kind of reasons, too... People like the Altiers.

The house wasn't what he'd been expecting. It was pretty, a log cabin set back in the woods at the crest of a mountain. The isolated location was particularly creepy, though, as he considered the dangerous drop he knew was right behind the house and the dense woods where a family could hide with shotguns. That last part had actually happened when Alanna's real sister had come searching for her and almost died in the process.

When police and the FBI had gone through the house after the Altiers had been arrested, they'd found a stash of forged documents. They'd also found years' worth of family pictures. According to police gossip, the earliest pictures showed obviously distraught kids, but as time went by, that changed. The pictures started to show what looked like a happy family. The most disturbing thing of all, according to one of the Desparre police department's veterans, was how much they'd all looked like a real family. Apparently the Altiers had grabbed kids who looked like they were related. The veteran had confided in Peter that what haunted him most was that if Alanna hadn't left the note, no one would ever look at the seven people living in this house and think for a second they weren't a legitimate family.

To Peter, the scariest part was how that lie still seemed lodged in the mind of the person who had been the least brainwashed, the one who'd ultimately turned the kidnappers in.

Still, rumor had it that the Altiers had learned from their mistakes—when two of the kids they'd kidnapped couldn't forget their real families, they had started abducting younger children. It appeared that Darcy was sticking to that pattern, because police believed she'd grabbed a three-year-old boy not long after she'd escaped custody.

"Let's see where Alanna is headed next," Peter muttered. He was normally good at stakeouts, at making sure no one spotted him or his vehicle in a town full of naturally suspicious residents. It was a skill he'd learned as a reporter, when he'd sometimes go on scouting missions with soldiers. When he'd needed to keep up and keep quiet. But apparently the Altiers had taught Alanna to be hypervigilant and wary of strangers, and to run at the first indication someone might have noticed her.

It was ironic, really, that she still lived by that credo. After being plucked out of her front yard by a stranger as a kid, she should have been hypervigilant in a totally different way. Crowds should have been a source of comfort—more people to notice if something went wrong. Instead, she was still following what she'd been taught by the couple who'd kidnapped her and hidden her away from the world.

All of those things told Peter where her allegiance still lay. It was obvious to him that when it came to a choice between helping bring Darcy in—the line she'd given the police—and helping her escape, she'd choose the latter. Most likely, she'd do it regardless of the cost to others.

His hand was halfway to his left ear before he realized and yanked it back down.

"We need to be objective here," Tate said, somehow sensing what Peter was thinking.

Peter hadn't told Tate about his experiences overseas, but his last assignment as a war reporter was something few people in and around his hometown had missed. It had made national papers—along with a picture of him, blood dripping from his head, a cloud of dust covering his entire body and a stunned look on his face. The cameraman who'd caught the shot had done so seconds before the horrific aftermath of what Peter had just seen, what he'd just experienced. Only later would Peter realize most of the hearing in his left ear was never going to return.

"What we need to do is keep her in our sight," Peter grumbled, following the tire tracks in the loose snow. This far on the outskirts of Desparre, the roads saw minimal traffic. People who lived out this way all had snowmobiles for days when the snow got too deep for driving.

"It didn't look like anyone had been at the Altier house in a long time," Tate continued, unperturbed or indifferent that Peter was annoyed. "Don't you think if Darcy and Alanna had been in touch, Alanna would have known where to go? It seems like she's guessing as much as we are."

"Well, maybe they haven't been in touch. Or maybe they have and all Alanna knows is that Darcy is coming back to Desparre."

"If Alanna really wanted to help Darcy, why would she stop by the police station and offer us her help? Until she did that, no one was looking for Darcy here."

Peter let up on the gas slightly as Tate's words sank in. The search for the kidnapped boy—and escaped felon Darcy Altier—was making national news, but the search itself was centralized in Oregon. If anyone in law enforcement had reason to think Darcy was coming here, no one at their station seemed to know it.

Peter frowned and pressed down on the gas pedal again, hoping he was still following the right tire tracks but not willing to get within visual distance of Alanna's vehicle. Not willing to risk scaring her off again. She might have left five years ago, but when it came to the most remote part of Desparre, she definitely knew it better than he did.

"Where's she going?" Tate asked, his quiet tone suggesting he was talking to himself more than Peter.

"No idea," Peter answered anyway. "A second meetup point maybe?"

Tate shook his head and Peter could sense he was rolling his eyes. "I know Desparre isn't exactly a hotbed of crime and no one is likely to be missing us right now, but I seriously doubt Alanna Morgan came all this way, knocked on the police's door and gave us a heads-up she thinks Darcy is here, then headed right to her."

"Maybe not," Peter conceded. "But she's obviously searching for Darcy. And no one in Desparre knows her better."

"Okay," Tate agreed. "It still seems unlikely that Darcy would run back to Desparre, but if she *is* here, Alanna has a better shot at finding her than any of us."

"Glad you're seeing it my way," Peter said with a grin as he wound around another steep bend, taking them farther up the mountain. He cranked up the heater, feeling the temperature dropping as they climbed.

"If Alanna actually does find Darcy, she might need our help," Tate said.

"Why's that?"

"She's the reason Darcy Altier spent the last five years in prison. She's the reason Julian Altier died in prison."

"I don't think we can pin all of that on Alanna." Despite his suspicions about her motives now, she wasn't responsible for their actions or what had happened to them. It must have taken enormous fortitude to eventually turn them in. He had to give her that.

"I'm talking about Darcy's perspective, Peter. Alanna might think the woman who raised her will be happy to see her and will hand over this kid, but honestly? I think she's just as likely to take a shot at Alanna like she did at her sister five years ago."

Peter frowned, the idea of Alanna Morgan facing down a shotgun making him push the gas pedal harder. But when he rounded another bend, the road ended. A big wooden sign half-buried in snow announced it a dead end.

He hit the brakes hard and the SUV skidded to a stop, the four-wheel drive groaning. He glanced around, searching for a trail that snaked off somewhere, but saw nothing. "Where did she go?"

Tate shook his head, a hint of a smile on his lips. "I think she's a lot savvier than we gave her credit for. We lost her."

Chapter Three

"Hey, Chief, have you talked to Colter Hayes lately?" Peter asked as he strode back into the police station's bullpen the next day, Tate on his heels.

Chief Hernandez frowned back at him, disapproval in the lines between her eyebrows.

Peter had met Keara Hernandez when he had applied for the police officer position but knew little about her. In a town where people respected others' right to privacy, she hadn't shared much of her background with her officers. All Peter knew was that she'd come from somewhere in the Lower 48, where she'd been a detective. The move to the remote town of Desparre was a chance for a promotion, sure, but they didn't see much crime here. Undoubtedly, she was running from something—like so many of their civilians—but Peter had found her to be a fair boss. Her one shortcoming was her tendency to cut off ideas she didn't like, shutting them down fast.

He could see it coming before she opened her mouth, so he preempted her with another question. "When's the last time Colter was in Desparre with Alanna's sister?"

Colter Hayes was a Desparre transplant, a soldier who'd seen his entire unit die and decided to spend the rest of his life in the solitude of Desparre. Then he'd met Kensie Morgan and eventually followed her back to Chicago. But first, he'd helped Kensie track down Alanna—and in the process, uncovered the Altiers' kidnapping scheme.

The chief crossed her arms over her chest, turning to face him from where she'd been standing in front of the station's overworked coffeepot. "I've had some contact with him. He hasn't been back in about a year now. His wife is pregnant. Actually…" Chief Hernandez's eyes lifted upward, then she nodded. "No, by now, they've had the baby. I'm guessing they're pretty busy back in Chicago."

"Because—"

She cut him off with a single dismissive word, spoken with authority. "No, Peter."

Despite the fact that she was only six years older than his twenty-nine years, she said his name the way his mom had when he got in trouble as a boy. It made him feel like a kid and he scowled. He might have way more experience as a reporter than a police officer, but he knew how to follow a lead. And Alanna Morgan was a lead.

"Alanna Morgan was a *victim*," Chief Hernandez said. "It's sad that she can't let go of her past, but it's not our problem. I've talked to the federal agents handling the investigation back in Oregon and there's no reason to suspect Darcy Altier came this way."

"Is there a reason to suspect she went anywhere else?"

Chief Hernandez gave him an exasperated sigh, her gaze darting once to Tate, who stayed silent, then back to Peter. "What is this fixation with the Altiers? I didn't assign you to look into this. Alanna is on a mission for herself, Peter. She probably feels guilty for everything that happened, even if it wasn't her fault. She wants to help, but she's out here guessing. It's our job to make sure she's safe while she's here. But she's not a lead worth following. Leave her alone."

"What if she's right?"

"I already—"

"Alanna didn't fly all this way for nothing. Sure, maybe she does feel guilty, but if she thought Darcy was still in Oregon, wouldn't she go there?"

"Peter, this woman isn't law enforcement. She doesn't have any insight into this case that we don't."

"She does have insight into Darcy Altier that we don't," Tate contributed.

Peter glanced at his partner, who was leaning against the wall, looking unruffled by the argument with the chief. But Tate didn't feel as strongly about Alanna being a lead. He definitely didn't have as much to prove as Peter.

Giving him a quick nod of thanks for the support, Peter turned back to the chief. "Maybe Darcy Altier isn't here. But maybe she's on her way. I've read through the case information and Desparre is the only place the couple stayed for more than a year. Darcy got comfortable here. If anywhere is home to her, it's our town."

Chief Hernandez's forehead creased and her eyes narrowed, like she was thinking over his argument. Then she shook her head. "Whatever we don't know about the Altiers' motivations or mindsets, we can say this—those kids felt loved. The Altiers raised them like they were really their own children. That couple created a makeshift family for themselves. She and her husband got away with it for eighteen years, from the time they kidnapped that first boy until they were caught. They're not stupid. They know their house was searched and ultimately seized. She's not coming back here, Peter. And I won't waste your time—or Tate's time—following Alanna Morgan around."

"This isn't five years ago, Chief," Peter insisted. He thought of Alanna racing to the street to get a look at his SUV back at the Altier cabin. The expectation on her face, the hope that had shifted into wariness as he'd reversed at high speed.

Alanna believed the woman she'd called mom for fourteen years was returning to Desparre. That meant Peter believed it, too.

"That image of a happy family was all an illusion," Peter reminded her. "I'm not saying they didn't love those kids, in their own messed-up way. But Darcy and Julian made Desparre their hideout. In the end, this place destroyed them. Darcy spent five years in jail. Her husband died there. She watched all her 'kids' being taken away. This time around, do you really think she'd repeat those mistakes?"

The chief's arms dropped from where they'd been crossed over her chest for most of the conversation. Reluctant interest sparked in her eyes. "Wouldn't coming back to Desparre be a mistake, then?"

"That assumes she's thinking straight. She could be operating on pure emotion. Wanting what she had, where she had it. Or wanting something else, something stronger. Maybe this time, her goal isn't to steal herself a new family."

"Except she's already started one, with that little three-year-old boy in Oregon," Tate argued. But even he had pushed away from the wall and stepped closer, looking more interested in the conversation.

"Maybe the plan isn't to start a new family with this little boy. After all, where's the rest of Darcy's 'family'? Dead. Or back with their real families. Maybe this time, she's out to prove something."

"What?" Chief Hernandez asked, but the question was less hostile now.

"That she can outwit us all. Maybe Alanna's right, in a way. Maybe Darcy is coming back here to get revenge on us. The town that gave her up."

Chief Hernandez's lips twisted upward in the corners, but she was nodding slowly. "Except it wasn't really Desparre who turned Darcy in. It was Alanna."

"Exactly," Peter said. "Which means if Alanna isn't in on Darcy's escape, she might be a target."

Tate stepped a little closer. "So, you think we need to keep following her, to keep her safe?" he asked, probably assuming this was Peter's roundabout way to keep chasing that lead.

"Sure," Peter said. "That's one reason to keep following her."

"What's the other?" Chief Hernandez asked, eyes narrowing like she already knew the answer.

"She's our bait to catch a kidnapper."

"ALANNA?" THE HIGH-PITCHED voice gained volume and then a hand gripped Alanna's arm hard. "Alanna Morgan?"

Reluctantly, Alanna turned to face the woman with long blond hair and perfect makeup who'd stopped her as she and Chance stepped out of their truck in the parking lot of Jasper's General Store. The store where Alanna had left her fateful note five years ago.

"I thought it was you," the woman said, her voice too cheery, her eyes too bright. Her breath swirled between them in the cold, doing nothing to obscure the raw ambition in her gaze.

No doubt about it. She might not have a microphone or a camera crew, but she was a reporter.

Alanna had been here for twenty-four hours and already a reporter had found her.

From the way Chance let out a low rumble—not quite a growl, but not friendly—when she reached her hand toward Alanna, he knew it, too.

The woman withdrew her hand quickly, her too-huge smile slipping just a bit, and Alanna felt herself being transported back five years.

The flight home had seemed to take forever. She'd been heading to a suburb outside of Chicago, to a home she'd never seen because her parents had long since moved out of the place where she'd been kidnapped in the front yard. Clutching Kensie's hand too hard on the turbulent flight, having never been on an airplane before. Nerves churning her stomach as she prepared to greet parents and a brother she hadn't seen in fourteen long years.

The drive from the airport to her parents' house, where she'd soon be living, had gone by in a blur but the moments afterward were the ones Alanna would never forget. She'd expected her parents and brother, had known their extended family was waiting to give them a private reunion first. They didn't want to overwhelm her, they said.

But she hadn't expected the reporters. The news vans had made it nearly impossible for their driver to pull up to the house. The bursts of light from camera flashes going off all around her had made it hard to see. The reporters and their crews had pushed in on her from all sides, making her feel claustrophobic. Their questions screamed at her from all directions. *What's it like being home after all these years? Do you remember your real family? Did the Altiers hurt you? Why did you leave that note? Why didn't you come forward sooner?*

Trying to shake off the memories, Alanna leveled the woman with a hard stare and pulled her arm free. "No comment."

Five years ago, Kensie had snapped those words at the reporters, pulled Alanna protectively into the crook of her arm and propelled her forward into the respective quiet of the house. Inside, Alanna had immediately been folded into hugs by her parents, while her teary-eyed older brother stared at her in wonder.

Of course she'd known they would have changed

in fourteen years. Just as she'd changed from a curly-haired five-year-old into a young woman.

Still, it had been a shock to see the streaks of gray in her mother's dark hair, the worry lines on her father's forehead and at the corners of his eyes. The scents of her father's aftershave and her mother's perfume had swirled around her, subtle but still making her eyes water—she was used to the outdoorsy scents of the Altiers when they hugged her. Her parents had looked older than their years. Alanna had been struck with the guilt of realizing it was probably from having their youngest child ripped out of their lives, from the years of searching and always coming up empty.

Then there was Flynn, standing stock-still, his lips trembling as his tears started to spill at the corners of his eyes. It had been hard to reconcile the twenty-three-year-old man staring at her with the nine-year-old brother she remembered. He'd been thinner than she'd expected and there was something desperate in his gaze she realized only later had come from years of bad decisions and addictions he'd fought hard to break. He had started when he was a teenager, feeling neglected by parents who'd been constantly looking for the daughter they'd lost, forgetting the two children they still had left.

All of it, ultimately leading back to her. To all the small moments over the years that were chances she might have had to reach out sooner, but hadn't taken. There hadn't been a lot, but she'd definitely had opportunities. In the beginning, she'd been far too afraid to take them. As she grew up, as she grew to love the family she lived with, she'd been scared of what it would mean for all of them.

In the early years with the Altiers, she used to squeeze her eyes closed tight and hold the images of her family in her mind, desperate not to lose them. As she'd grown, those images had blurred around the edges. Memories had faded, leaving behind only vague images and the feeling of having once been loved by a totally different family. With fourteen years between them missing, the homecoming she'd expected to be joyous had been happy but awkward. At that moment, the idea of rebuilding a life she barely remembered with a family she'd only known as a young child had seemed overwhelming.

"Are you sure?"

The reporter's voice cut through her memories and Alanna realized she'd frozen in the parking lot while the woman stared at her quizzically.

As Alanna's gaze refocused, the woman rushed on, "No one's ever really told your side of the story. What it was like to say goodbye to four kids you'd considered your brothers and sisters. What it was like to go home to a family you hadn't seen since you were five. I can do that for you."

Alanna's gut clenched at the reporter's insight, but she shook her head and turned away, rushing for the store with Chance keeping pace. She didn't take a full breath again until she was inside with the door closed behind her.

Here, at least, things looked the same. She'd been inside Jasper's General Store only a few times over the years they'd lived in Desparre. The Altiers had feared someone would recognize her, even years later and so many thousands of miles from where she'd been kidnapped. But as time went on, she'd eventually been given more freedom.

Trailing her hands over the rusting metal shelves filled with household staples, Alanna walked slowly toward the counter where an old man sat. The owner, Jasper. The man Julian had asked her to hand over the money to for their groceries. The man who'd unknowingly taken the note within her stack of cash.

He stood as she approached, recognition in his deep brown eyes. His gaze flicked once to Chance, walking happily along beside her, then returned to her. "Alanna Morgan."

"Hi." She stuffed her gloved hands into the pockets in her coat. "I was wondering—you knew my... Julian Altier once. Did you know Darcy?"

Jasper had a reputation for being cranky and unapproachable, and as he came around the counter, his pace was slow but determined. But when he stopped in front of her, there was compassion in his gaze and sadness in his voice. "I didn't really know either of them. I'd only seen Julian a few times over the years. I'm sorry I never noticed anything wrong. I wasn't even sure how that note got into my stack of cash."

Alanna shook her head, squeezed the hand he'd reached toward her. "It's not your fault. Even when I handed over the money and the note, I didn't act like anything was wrong." In some ways, nothing had been wrong. In others, everything had been.

"So you wouldn't recognize Darcy if she came through here?"

His eyes narrowed, making more lines crease his weather-worn skin. "I'd recognize her now, of course, with all the media coverage. But back then? I don't know. She might have come through here with Julian before, once or twice over the years. Hard to say."

"But not recently?" Alanna pressed, trying not to get discouraged.

"No way. People around here would know her now. We'd turn her in."

He said it like it was exactly what Alanna would want to hear, but her shoulders dropped. Maybe the police were right. The people in Desparre felt betrayed by Julian and Darcy, were angry with all the negative attention the couple had brought them. If there was any place Darcy would be recognized quickly, it was an insular town that promised anonymity but recognized and distrusted anyone who didn't live here.

"Thanks," Alanna said, her voice coming out in a squeak. She saw Jasper's lips twist in sympathy as she spun toward the door.

"Come on, Chance," she said as her St. Bernard lagged slightly behind, probably wondering what they were doing.

She'd been a fool to come here, to think she could make a difference. A fool to think that Darcy would return to the place that had once made her most happy, instead of doing what she'd been truly doing all along: running.

Alanna had been a fool to risk the bonds she'd spent

five years rebuilding with her family to chase after her kidnapper.

Shame and anger filled her as she pushed the door open a little too hard, almost slamming into someone.

The "sorry" died on her lips as the person on the other side caught the door and flung it the rest of the way open.

Then he was filling the doorway with his scowl, the gaze of his too-blue eyes drilling into her. Peter Robak. The cop who thought she was in cahoots with Darcy.

Only after she'd slipped away from the SUV following her yesterday—making a quick turn onto a wide path not meant as a road—had she realized who was chasing her. Not a threat like she'd imagined, a pair of men who'd spotted a woman all by herself in an isolated area. But police officers who thought she was little better than a criminal.

"You can stop following me around now," she snapped at him, taking an aggressive step forward despite knowing it was a bad idea to get inside a cop's personal space. But the fear she'd felt yesterday shifted into fury now. The shame and guilt and frustration felt better channeling outward than inward. "I'm finished here, okay? You can leave me alone."

From the corner of her eye, she saw Peter's partner—the other man in the SUV yesterday. Surprise was on his face, his hand dropping away from his weapon as if he'd reached for it when he saw someone rush toward Peter, then changed his mind when he saw it was just her. Just a foolish woman chasing a past that was better left alone.

"You're leaving?" he asked.

But it was Peter's words that drew all of her attention: "You were right."

Dread dropped into her stomach. "Right about what?" Was Darcy here after all? Had someone spotted her?

People here were often armed, ready to protect their own when help could be far away. The residents understood that Desparre usually attracted people who just wanted solitude, but that it could also attract those trying to escape something they'd done, something that had the law chasing them. Had one of those people seen Darcy and taken aim? Had the police arrested her? "What happened?"

Peter frowned at her, studying her like he was trying to unravel all of her secrets, all of the years she had spent happily living with a pair of kidnappers, then turning them in one day. "Darcy's not in Desparre. Not yet. But I think she's on her way."

"What? Why?"

A slight smile twisted one side of his lips, but there was nothing happy about it. "We know she's headed in this direction from Oregon."

"Why?" Alanna pressed, every second she stood there waiting to understand adding to her anxiety, making her stomach churn and her breathing turn shallow.

Chance let out a low whine and nudged her with his nose.

She put a hand on his head, stroking his fur to assure him she was okay, even if it wasn't true.

"She was spotted in Canada today. They didn't catch

her, but now this has become an international chase, Alanna."

Alanna sensed Peter's partner stepping closer, as if he planned to intervene in whatever Peter was going to say next, but she couldn't take her gaze off Peter.

He stared back at her, his uncompromising expression only cracking as he said, "Darcy kidnapped another kid today."

Chapter Four

"What's Darcy's endgame?"

Peter's words were angry and suddenly he was the one getting into her personal space.

Alanna backed up a step and Chance pushed his way between her and the police officer, using his size and St. Bernard strength as a warning.

"Chance," Alanna said, tugging his collar just enough to let him know he should back up, too. But her mind was still trying to get a grip on the words Peter had spoken a moment ago.

Darcy was partway between where she'd escaped custody and Desparre. Now she had two kidnapped kids with her instead of one.

"It makes no sense."

She didn't realize she'd spoken the words out loud until Peter asked, "What? How many kids does this woman have to kidnap before you see her as a threat, as a criminal?"

Anger made her heat up underneath her winter gear and she could feel the flush rising to her cheeks.

"Peter," his partner said, his voice quiet but firm. "Go easy."

Then he stuck a hand toward her. "I'm Officer Tate Emory. I was in the police station yesterday when you came in to offer your help. We'd like to take you up on that."

He was the officer she'd noticed watching her exchange with the chief from the bullpen yesterday. Her eyes narrowed as she looked from him to Peter. "Why? Because now you know I can lose you when you follow me around?"

Tate's lips twitched, like he was holding back amusement.

Peter took a step closer. "Because it's the right thing to do." His tone was less raw anger now, more accusatory, as if daring her to say she *wouldn't* help the police.

The police had scoffed at her offer before. Then they had two officers follow her around like she was a criminal. And now?

She wasn't sure how Darcy would feel seeing her again. But she figured the woman was way more likely to let her get close if she was alone than if she had a pair of police officers trailing her every move. Especially police officers Alanna didn't trust.

Peter might say helping them was the right thing to do, but how could she believe they'd do what was right when the time came? Would they trust her to talk Darcy into turning herself in, into turning over the kids she'd kidnapped, rather than run or fight? She doubted it.

"I think you ought to leave her alone."

The voice came from behind her. When Alanna

glanced over her shoulder, she saw Jasper scowling at the cops, his arms crossed over his chest.

She gave him a thankful, shaky smile before Tate drew her attention again.

"Look, we should have been up front with you," he said, giving Peter a glare that clearly said *go easy.* "We didn't have any reason to believe Darcy was coming here before. Now we do. And you have insight into the places she knows in and around Desparre. You have insight into her as a person. You can help us bring those kids home to their families."

She stared back at him, at the guileless look on his face, and saw something else there. Not the distrust Peter broadcasted whenever he spoke to her, but pity.

Averting her gaze, she felt a familiar discomfort well up. The feel of too many eyes on her, all evaluating, all judging. Not just reporters, but also all the people who read or watched their stories. To this day, she still got mail from some of them, letters of encouragement or morbid curiosity or misplaced anger.

She was sick of all of it.

Forcing her gaze back up, she told both officers, "I was wrong. I don't think I can help you. But if I find anything, I'll let you know."

She wasn't sure if the last words were a lie or not.

"Alanna—"

Peter stepped closer still, despite Chance angled protectively in front of her.

Chance let out another low warning growl, but Peter only glanced at him, seemingly unconcerned. Apparently he recognized that the St. Bernard wouldn't hurt anyone unless they were a real threat to her.

"This isn't like Darcy," Alanna admitted, the words breaking free before she'd even realized she thought them.

It was true. The Altiers had gone years between grabbing kids. Abducting two within a few days, while on the run from the law, was reckless.

Was Darcy trying to create a brand-new, ready-made family? Did she want to re-create what she'd had with Alanna and her "siblings"? Had she simply snapped from the grief of her husband's death, after years being locked away, after losing the kids she'd raised?

It was possible. And yet, something didn't seem right. It didn't seem like Darcy at all.

"Are we sure she's the one who took those kids?" Alanna looked from Peter to Tate, trying to read the truth in their eyes because she wasn't sure she'd hear it from their lips.

The pity intensified on Tate's face, in the way his lips crumpled, in the tilt of his head.

Peter just looked exasperated. "What do you think? That someone else is following her—an escaped fugitive—and they just happen to be doing what she did for eighteen years? Really?"

"No," Alanna said softly, because it sounded ridiculous. Obviously it was Darcy. But if she was acting this out of character, even if Alanna could find her, would she be able to get through to her? Would she be able to change anything? Or was coming here a total waste of time?

THE DOOR TO their old home had been left unlocked. It opened with a hard shove, groaning in a way that told Alanna no one had been through in a long time. She slipped underneath the faded yellow tape that had probably once read Do Not Cross but had become illegible over five Alaskan winters.

Her heart began to pound as she stepped over the threshold and a thousand memories hit her at once. Darcy and Julian sitting side by side, holding hands on the blue couch Darcy had upholstered herself. Alanna's older "brother" Johnny staring at the chessboard in the corner, contemplating his next move in a long-running game with Julian. Her younger "siblings" Sydney and Drew sitting cross-legged on the floor, teaching their youngest "sister" Valerie to make a pair of snowshoes.

After Darcy and Julian had been arrested, Johnny had stared at her with disbelief and confusion. In all the years since, he'd refused to speak to her. Five years of Alanna's letters had been returned unopened. Yet at least once a year, Alanna still tried.

Sydney, three years younger than Alanna and the "sibling" she'd always felt closest to, had tried to keep in touch. In the beginning, she and Alanna had spoken on the phone almost nightly. Slowly, though, the frequency of those calls had decreased, until now Alanna only heard from her every few weeks.

Alanna stomped her feet on the heavy rug still lining the entryway as Chance pushed his way in beside her, knocking free one end of the police tape. The broken tape immediately blew outward, dancing in the wind.

Alanna shut the door behind it, closing out the frigid wind and falling snow.

Beside her, Chance did a full-body shake, sending melted snow everywhere. Then he walked into the main room as if he'd been there a hundred times and settled in front of the dark fireplace. It was as if he knew this place had once been her home and he felt at home here, too.

She followed more slowly, each step farther into the house feeling as if she was stepping backward in time. As she ran her hand over the soft, worn blanket on the corner of the sofa, she could picture Drew and Valerie curled underneath it, one on each end of the couch, their toes meeting in the middle.

She'd tried to keep in touch with them, too, but their parents had cut off all contact when they'd gone home. Drew would turn eighteen next year, which meant Alanna could try again. But Valerie was only eleven. By the time she was an adult, how much of her time with Alanna would she remember? Valerie had been six when the Altier "family" had been broken apart—only a year older than Alanna when she'd been kidnapped. Had her memories of Alanna already blurred around the edges, the same way Alanna's had of the Morgans over the years?

The "siblings" she'd spent the majority of her childhood with were now scattered across the country, no two in the same state. Her video chats with Sydney were the closest she'd come to seeing any of them since that day when police had stopped their car and screamed at her "parents" to get out.

Alanna blinked back tears that suddenly flooded her

vision. She wasn't here to wallow in regrets or wonder if she'd made the right choice five years ago. She was here for clues.

It had been two days since Darcy was spotted in northern Canada, since she'd grabbed another young child, this time a two-year-old girl. According to news reports, there had been no confirmed sightings of her since.

Two days ago, after talking to Peter and Tate, Alanna had been ready to head home. Yesterday, she'd even packed her small suitcase and looked for flights. She'd finally picked up one of the calls from her sister Kensie, promising she'd be heading home on Saturday. Instead, today, she'd texted Kensie that she was staying a little longer. She might not be able to talk Darcy down as she'd planned, but she could still help. If anyone could find Darcy now, it was Alanna.

The problem was, if Darcy was speeding back to Alaska, kidnapping more kids along the way, it meant five years in prison had definitely changed her. But not in the way Alanna had expected.

Throughout her childhood, Alanna had always seen Darcy as the "parent" who was the dreamer. Easily distracted, always lost in her own thoughts, she had a million ideas but rarely the initiative to see them all through. It was Julian who took her ideas and made them reality.

All through the house were examples of the way her "parents" had fit together, worked together. The fireplace, for instance, with its border of colorful tiles, had started as an idea Darcy had sketched out to resemble the aurora borealis at night. But it was Julian who'd purchased those tiles, taught all of them to affix them to the fireplace. Darcy had envisioned the extra room toward the back of the house as a place to homeschool and Julian had found schoolbooks for all of them. Then, of course, there were the kidnappings.

Alanna hugged her arms around herself, cold despite being out of the wind and snow. But the heat was off in the house, her breath making cloud puffs in the air.

One of the clearest memories she had—the memory that still woke her in the middle of the night—was that moment when Julian had reached out from his car and yanked her inside. Darcy had been at the wheel, speeding away dangerously as Alanna yelped in surprise and fright, squirming to look out the rear window. She had watched Kensie get smaller in the distance, even as her sister ran after their vehicle, screaming for help.

When Alanna was taken, the Altiers had already had Johnny for four years. Even then, Johnny had barely remembered his birth family and he'd already adjusted to living with the Altiers. The four of them had moved constantly in those early years, never staying in one place too long.

Alanna had only been five years old then, totally reliant on three people she didn't trust. Peter was probably right that being so dependent on them from such a young age had helped forge a deeper connection. Slowly, Alanna's fear and hatred had shifted. Her "parents" and "brother" had worn her down with love and caring. As guilty as she'd felt about it, she'd started to care for them, too.

By the time they'd grabbed Sydney, Alanna hadn't

forgotten the Morgans. But she'd felt like she had a new family.

That was when she'd learned how the kidnappings worked. Darcy and Julian always talked about wanting a big family, but apparently Darcy couldn't get pregnant. Every few years, Darcy would see a kid—one who looked like an Altier—and felt as if the child was already hers. Then Julian would make it a reality.

Darcy doing the kidnappings without Julian seemed so counter to the way her "mother" worked. Alanna had come here thinking she could talk some sense into her, make her realize her actions were emotional and unethical. But abducting *two* kids, in such a short span of time? It meant Darcy was different now, that she was taking on both hers and Julian's past parental roles. It meant she wasn't the person Alanna remembered.

When Alanna was a child, she'd always been able to talk Darcy into things to make her happy. One more story at bedtime. A warmer pair of boots so she could spend more time playing in the snow. A later bedtime so she could stay up reading or playing games with her "siblings." But now? With everything that had changed while Darcy was in jail? Would Alanna be able to interrupt Darcy's plan?

Shutting out the memories along with worries of what would happen if she *did* find Darcy, Alanna took a deep breath and looked around the room. Chance had gotten up without her noticing and was standing next to her, staring up at her with those dark brown eyes. A string of drool in the corner of his droopy mouth nearly stretched to the wooden floor and made Alanna smile.

She stroked his soft fur, then said, "Let's get to work."

His head swiveled, as if taking in the small front room and asking, *Doing what?*

"We're looking for somewhere else Darcy could hide," Alanna told him.

He tilted his head at her, making the drool break free, and Alanna laughed. It loosened the tension in her chest, was the impetus she needed to get moving.

Five years ago, when Kensie had shown up at their house searching for her, Darcy and Julian had bundled all the kids quickly into the car and fled. Alanna had initially thought they were going back to what they'd done years ago, skipping from state to state, hiding. Then she'd learned Julian had a specific hiding place in mind and it was nearby. They'd never made it, though, because the police had caught up to them. As far as Alanna knew, other property owned by the Altiers—in their name or some other name—had never been uncovered. But that didn't mean it didn't exist.

If Darcy was returning to Desparre, it was unlikely she'd come back to the cabin. That was too dangerous. But some other hiding spot her husband had scoped out years ago that police and the FBI had never uncovered? That seemed reasonable.

Alanna didn't know where it was. But there had to be a clue in this cabin. She walked from room to room slowly, her gaze lighting on every object, all the pieces of their lives that had been left behind. She picked up old books, looked through cupboards now littered with rodent droppings and then retraced her steps, trying to see it all anew.

Two hours later, she held a small piece of paper in her hand. She'd found it taped to the inside cover of one of Darcy's old drawing books. If the police had found it five years ago, apparently they hadn't thought anything of the random symbols. But they meant something to Alanna: a goofy code she and her "siblings" had created one particularly frigid winter when they'd all been stuck inside for two weeks. Darcy had encouraged them, laughing as they'd constructed what they thought was a tightly encrypted cipher. Translated, the symbols in Darcy's book were a series of latitudes and longitudes. Coordinates.

Alanna stared at the list, five places she knew in her gut were hiding spots. Then she looked over at Chance. "Let's start at the top."

Chance must have felt the mix of excitement and anxiety in her words because he got to his feet quickly and chased her to the door. When she flung it open, her excitement transitioned immediately to dread.

The snow that had been falling slowly for the past few hours had picked up intensity, racing faster for the ground, piling on top of the foot and a half's worth that had already come down over the past two days. Alanna squinted at the gray sky, then at the truck she'd rented. It was built for off-roading in the Alaskan terrain. But there was no rental vehicle hardy enough for the furious climate Desparre could spawn.

In November, conditions could turn dangerous fast. Alanna checked the weather app on her phone, which indicated that the snow was supposed to stop before the top of the hour, only a few minutes away. As if she'd willed it, when she looked back up, the speed of the falling snow had decreased, the snowflakes seeming to shrink in size.

"I think we can do it," she told Chance, glancing again at the paper in her hand. According to her navigation app, the first location was less than half an hour's drive. And she'd spent years in the unpredictable Desparre weather, understood how to take care of herself in it.

Chance bolted out the door, bounding in circles in the fresh snow before coming to a stop by the back door of the truck. He glanced back at her, as if to say, *What are you waiting for?*

She hurried after him, slower in the heavy snow, and opened the truck door for him.

Chance leaped into the back seat, bringing snow with him and making Alanna wish she'd brought more towels.

She ran to the front, turning the heat up to high as soon as she was inside. Tucking the paper into the inside pocket of her coat, she eased the truck carefully out of the driveway, happy to see that the snowfall was slowing even more.

Still, the roads near the cabin were unpaved. The town didn't bother to clear them and the people who lived out this way all had snowmobiles for when winter got too tough for even their all-weather vehicles. So, Alanna drove slowly and carefully, following in other tire tracks where she could. She headed farther away from Desparre, but down the mountain this time, on roads that wound around massive old trees.

It was the route they'd been on five years ago, when the police had caught up to them.

Snow shot out from beneath the tires, fluffy stuff that would have been perfect for building snowmen. Luckily, there was no ice underneath it. On one side of her, the mountain continued upward; on the other was the cliff edge.

She gripped the wheel tightly, slightly less confident after five years of living near Chicago, with their milder winters, snow removal services, far-reaching cell towers and easy access to help. She glanced in her rearview mirror at Chance, lying across the back seat, but his head up, watching out the window. He met her gaze in the mirror, trusting, and she wondered if she was making a mistake.

But when she glanced at her navigation app, she realized she'd driven farther than she'd expected. The snow had stopped falling from the sky, but every once and a while, a big hunk of it slid off a tree branch, startling her as it plopped onto the windshield. She was close now. Her heart rate picked up in anticipation of finding the hideout Julian had probably built, at the possibility of finding Darcy there now.

Then she rounded a corner and swore as she stomped on the brake. The truck swerved slightly in the snow and Alanna clutched the wheel harder, angling away from the steep drop to her right.

Ahead of her, the road was blocked. A pile of snow higher than the front of her truck covered the entire road to the edge of the mountain. She couldn't tell how far it went, but as she leaned forward and glanced up through her windshield, she could tell why it had fallen. Avalanche.

"Guess we'll have to move on to the next spot," she

told Chance, but just as quickly, she decided to put that plan on hold. Where there'd been one avalanche, there could be another. Best to get away from the mountain and hope the snow melted.

She backed the truck up slowly, carefully as she got ready to round the bend again backward, since there was no room to turn around. But the tires slid on her anyway, and she overcorrected, more afraid of the drop-off than bumping the other side of the mountain. Except when her rear bumper hit the rock, the truck also slid into a rut. When she hit the gas again, the wheels spun, but the truck wouldn't go anywhere.

Cursing, Alanna pulled her hood over her head and hopped out of the truck to grab the shovel from the back. As soon as she stepped outside, a fierce shiver rushed through her body at the force of the wind. And as she opened the back door, Chance leaped out.

"No!" She made a grab for his collar even as he spun back toward her, but a noise overhead made her look up. A rumbling like thunder, but far too close. An avalanche.

Years of living in Alaska rushed back to her, as she stared at the mountaintop, instantly seeing the path of the snow. It would probably miss her if she backed away fast enough. But it was definitely going to take her truck. And Chance, standing too close to it…

She grabbed for him just as the wall of snow rushed downward, sweeping him up with it. Then her arms closed around him, just under his front legs. She clung tight, even as the snow slammed into her, hard and fast, shoving them both toward the edge of the mountain.

Chapter Five

Alanna Morgan knew something.

Peter had been following her around half the day. Unlike when he'd last followed her around with Tate three days ago, he was alone today. Saturday was his day off. Unfortunately, that meant he was in his personal vehicle instead of the police SUV. Although his truck could handle the Desparre winters, his police vehicle was equipped for anything. As Alanna headed farther away from Desparre, taking dangerous back roads down the mountain like she'd driven them a million times, Peter's knuckles went white gripping his steering wheel.

He'd grown up on the other side of the mountain, in an area almost as prone to crazy weather as Desparre. But the town of Luna—where his parents and older siblings lived still—was much flatter. They occasionally got nasty avalanches off this side of the mountain, but being at a lower altitude usually meant slightly fewer dangers. It definitely meant easier driving.

Since joining the Desparre police department last year, he'd been up on this mountain a few times, usually doing welfare checks. He'd driven it in far worse weather than this, but he'd never done it while chasing after a former victim, potential new accomplice or possible target. He'd never done it while trailing someone who seemed to know too well how to lose a tail.

Right now, she had good reason to try to lose him. Judging by the excitement on her face when she'd finally left the Altiers' cabin, she'd found something inside it. And the chances that she hadn't spotted him seemed low. So, when she rounded another corner and he heard snow crunching hard, as if she'd slammed the brakes, he eased off the side of the road and waited.

When her truck door slammed, he cursed and wedged his door open against the side of the mountain so he could climb awkwardly out of his vehicle. Better she stride over here, furious and ready for an argument than hide somewhere again while he drove past, clueless. But then she yelled "No!" and almost immediately—as if she'd been yelling at the mountain and it didn't want to listen—an ominous crash and boom signaled an oncoming avalanche.

His heart gave a quick, painful thud and then he was running toward her, rounding the corner before he could fully think it through.

Snow rushed downward from far above, a furious waterfall of white, slowing slightly along the road before it tumbled over the other side. There was a groan of metal over the rush of snow, only the top of Alanna's truck visible as it flipped sideways, then disappeared over the edge of the mountain.

Dread, anger and grief hit him unexpectedly hard. But he didn't have time to linger on it, because there she was, outside the vehicle, just a flash of her red coat in the flurry of snow.

He darted toward her and his left boot slid on the spilling snow, almost taking him down, sucking him under. He looked up quickly and saw that the avalanche was slowing, the end in sight way above him. But that flash of red was too close to the edge.

Fear threatened to freeze him in place, but he gritted his teeth and changed his angle, moving toward the edge of the mountain, toward a big old tree withstanding the onslaught of snow. Wrapping an arm and a leg around it, Peter reached out with his free hand, blindly now, since that flash of red had been overrun by snow.

Somehow, he grabbed her—or at least he hoped it was her. Cursing the thick gloves that made it hard to get a good grip, he clung to the edge of material. Then the snow yanked him forward, the pull hard and unrelenting, tearing at the socket in his shoulder.

The momentum ripped him around the front of the tree and the right side of his body burned with the contact. He clung to his quarry tighter, squeezing his left hand as tightly as he could, praying the coat wouldn't rip right out of his hand and take Alanna with it.

The snow shifted, taking a slight turn over the edge of the mountain, probably catching on the trees there. It pushed him back toward the big tree, easing the screaming pain in his shoulder and letting him get a better grip.

Suddenly, there she was, rising up on the curve of snow. First came her bright red coat, then a swash of long, dark, wet hair. Then her face, both too starkly pale and too bright red in places as she gasped for air.

"Your hand," he croaked, his voice lost beneath the still-thundering snow. He prayed she'd hear him, grab his arm and pull herself toward him.

If she replied, he couldn't hear it with his bad ear facing her. Instead, she tried to angle her body toward him in the snow and he saw both her arms wrapped underneath the front legs of her enormous dog. The St. Bernard was scrabbling for purchase with his huge paws and was actually managing to get a little traction, moving them both closer to Peter.

But then the last rush of snow swooped down and both of them disappeared underneath it.

Peter took a huge breath and squeezed his eyes shut as the snow claimed him, too.

She was suffocating.

The world around her finally stopped moving, but where had she landed? Had she tumbled over the edge of the mountain and managed to get wedged between some trees? Or was she still on the edge of the road, where one wrong move would send her flying over it?

She tried to move her fingers and felt Chance squirm in her arms. Tears pricked her eyes with the relief that he was still with her, still alive. But when she opened her eyes, there was only darkness. And cold like she'd never experienced.

The avalanche had buried them both. But how deeply?

She shifted along with Chance, not moving her arms from around his belly, not wanting him to go too far. Hoping there was a pocket of air, she finally had to open her mouth and gulp in a breath. There was a pocket, but it felt too little for both her and Chance, especially as her lungs demanded more, more, more.

Keeping one hand locked around Chance, she thrust the other upward, hoping to encounter fresh air. But there was only more snow. Was she really reaching up? Or had she been spun around so she thought down was up?

Don't panic, she reminded herself as her heart started thudding faster. She thrust her arm the other way, and this time she felt hard ground. At least, she thought so. Which meant escape was above her. But was it through a few feet of loosely packed snow, just above where her fingers could reach, or twelve feet deep and pressing down hard? Would movement help her get to safety or shift the weight of the snow so it crushed them both?

Her collapsible snow shovel was in her truck, which was probably buried under the snow with her. By the time she'd heard the telltale *whomp* of snow breaking free that signaled an oncoming avalanche, it had been too late. She should have known better; she never should have been out here in this weather. And now Chance, who'd suffered so much as a tiny puppy, who'd been her constant, loyal companion for the past two years, would probably die with her.

Stop it, she commanded herself. She needed to find a way out for both of them. For Peter, too?

Had she imagined seeing him at the edge of the avalanche in those brief moments when the snow had shifted and let her suck in a desperate lungful of air before it pulled her under again? Had she imagined his hand reaching out, yanking her backward, even as the avalanche tried to throw her forward, over the edge of the mountain? She reached behind her, felt a hand clutching her coat and her heart gave a hard thump.

He'd tried to save her. He didn't even like her, but he'd tried to save her life. Had it cost him his own?

The fingers locked in her coat weren't moving. She tried to scoot toward him, tried to urge Chance to come with her. She moved slowly, terrified of triggering more snow that might crush them, not sure how close they were to the edge of the mountain.

But as she slid toward Peter, Chance broke free from her grasp. She fumbled for him, her hands grasping nothing but snow, feeling clumsy in the cold.

"Chance!" As she gasped his name, she sucked in snow and more fell, closing the gap between her and her dog. She stretched her arms farther, but couldn't find him.

Panic took hold, squeezing her lungs tight as she turned her head and spit out the snow, trying to get more air. She found another pocket of it, but it felt stuffy, like it was already emptying of oxygen, and she tried to take shallow breaths. Reaching behind her, she tugged lightly on Peter's arm and he moved. But she couldn't tell if it was just gravity or if he was okay.

"Chance!" she tried again, even as she heard him moving away from her. Was he headed toward the edge of the mountain? She was too turned around to tell. Even if he managed to get free of the snow, would he fall over the edge?

Holding in a sob—for her dog, for herself, for Peter—

Alanna shifted again, sliding closer to Peter. She tried calling for Chance again, but she couldn't hear him anymore. She yelled louder, even as she wondered if she was doing the right thing. Maybe Chance could get free of the snow and save himself, at least.

Now, she had to try to do the same for her and Peter. As she scooted backward toward him through the heavy snow, his hand moved again, this time sliding down to grab her arm. Relief made more tears fill her eyes, but she blinked them back fast, not wanting them to freeze on her face.

She wasn't shivering so much anymore. Either she was adjusting to the cold or—more likely—she was starting to face hypothermia.

"We have to get out of here," she told Peter, even as the tiny pocket of air in front of her collapsed and more snow crashed down on her.

The weight felt crushing, the sudden lack of oxygen making her panic. She swung her arms out, trying to find a new pocket of air.

Then something scratched against her leg, a frantic pawing that got faster as she instinctively jerked away. Chance! He was trying to save her.

He was behind her now. Did that mean he'd somehow dug free of the avalanche? Alanna moved her legs, trying to help him free her. She grabbed Peter's hand as Chance suddenly took her ankle in his mouth and tugged.

She slid backward about a foot, snow crushing her even more, making her lungs and chest hurt. Then Chance's paws were up near her head and the snow in front of her face suddenly broke away, giving her precious air as the weight on her eased. She scooted toward him, trying to pull Peter with her, but Chance had already turned away from her.

He had started digging frantically beside her and soon Peter's torso and head emerged from the snow. Peter dropped her hand, somehow pulling himself forward, and then he and Chance were digging her the rest of the way out, dragging her free of the snow.

Struggling to her knees, Alanna threw shaky arms around Chance's back as she stared at the huge pile of snow. It was as tall as a house in the middle. Somehow, she, Peter and Chance had been at the edge of the avalanche, where it wasn't as high, where it hadn't smashed down hard enough to crush their bones or suffocate them. Her truck was gone, either buried under it or tossed over the side of the mountain, crashed somewhere below.

But she was alive. Chance was alive. And Peter was alive. That was all that mattered.

She stumbled to her feet and the bitter wind sliced through her wet clothes. Her teeth started chattering as Peter grabbed her hand.

"Come on. My truck's around the corner. We have to warm up."

As she stumbled after him, Chance at her side, Alanna realized his truck was far enough away that he could have avoided the avalanche altogether. He'd run toward it to save her, even though he didn't like her, even though he seemed to think she might be in cahoots with a kidnapper.

He didn't trust her. She didn't trust him, either. But he'd risked his life for her, which meant he was a good person. They might not agree on how to go about it, but they had the same ultimate goal: to save the kids Darcy had kidnapped.

They rounded the bend and Peter held open the door to his truck, waiting for her and Chance, his face a bright, unnatural red from the cold.

She slowed and he urged, "Come on, Alanna. Hurry."

"I want to work together," she blurted.

"What?"

It didn't matter what they thought of each other. She'd figure out a way to convince Peter that he needed to bring Darcy in carefully, peacefully. He had resources she didn't, like access to whatever the Desparre police learned from other law enforcement. But she had resources he needed, too, and an insight into Darcy's mindset that he'd never figure out without her.

They'd be stronger together.

"Let's work together to find Darcy and save those kids."

He stared at her a minute, something pensive in his brilliant blue eyes, then he nodded. "Deal. Now get in the truck."

Chapter Six

It was amazing they'd lived through the avalanche.

He wasn't sure he could handle another minute out in this cold. Instead of running around to the driver's side and trying to wedge the door open so close to the upward slant of the mountain, Peter clambered into his truck behind Alanna and Chance. His limbs were clumsy from the cold. He slammed the door shut behind him, pressing awkwardly against the dog until Chance leaped into the back to get out of the way. Then, Alanna scooted into the driver's seat, giving him a little space.

He'd left the truck running with the heat blasting, but he could barely feel it now. He turned it up all the way, then yanked off his sopping wet gloves. He reached up to take off his hat and discovered it was gone. His short hair was iced over and when he ran his hand through it, ice and water flew across the seat. Thrusting his hands in front of the heater, he glanced at Alanna, who'd slumped against the seat and closed her eyes.

"Come on," he told her and started unzipping her thick coat, which was definitely made for an Alaskan winter but not for getting buried in an avalanche. His fingers felt too big, swollen beyond their normal size and clumsy. But at least he could feel them, the stinging pain assuring him the nerves still worked.

"What are you doing?" she demanded, but the question had no heat. Her eyes opened, then drifted closed again.

"We've got to get out of these wet clothes," he muttered, running his tongue over his lip, which was way past chapped and split open as he spoke. "Come on," he said again, and this time, Chance pitched in.

The St. Bernard pressed his big head through the space between the seats and grabbed Alanna's sleeve with his mouth, tugging on it until she opened her eyes again.

She turned toward him sluggishly. "You okay, Chance?"

"He saved us," Peter said, giving the dog a quick pat on the head. "I guess he knows St. Bernards are snow rescue dogs."

Chance let go of Alanna's coat long enough to give a brief bark, which made Peter laugh and startled Alanna, finally seeming to focus her.

"It's so cold," she said, trying to tug the zipper back up on her coat.

"Nope." Peter ignored the squelch of his own uncomfortable, freezing clothes as he shifted to get closer to her. He yanked her gloves off and tossed them on the floor behind them, then awkwardly pulled off her coat. At least she could feel the cold. Her hands were bright red, which was definitely better than being unnaturally white, but they both needed to warm up fast.

Grunting at the uncomfortable angle and his aching body, he leaned over her and unlaced her boots, tugging them off her feet. Then came her thick socks. Her toes were too white and he rubbed them for a minute, then shoved her feet underneath the floor heaters.

When he came back up, she was shivering. A good sign.

"Get the rest of your clothes off," he said, slipping out of his own coat and dumping it on the floor behind him, careful not to drop it on Chance.

"Sorry, buddy," he said, leaning over the dog as he grabbed the stack of blankets he always kept in the vehicle in case of an emergency. Getting stalled out in Desparre could mean death if you weren't prepared.

He set most of the stack between him and Alanna, then tossed one over Chance, rubbing down the dog's back to dry some of the dampness.

Realizing Alanna was just staring at him, he yanked off his sweater and snapped, "Hurry up."

She flushed, a different shade of red flooding along her cheeks and neck, and quickly averted her gaze.

She was only five years younger than him, but he suddenly felt much older. He'd been inside war zones for years, lost most of the hearing in one ear and experienced huge change to his professional and personal life as a result. And her?

He realized he was still staring at her as she tried to cover herself with one of the blankets and shimmy out of her soaking jeans at the same time, so he turned the other way. Then he yanked off his boots and socks, sighing as the blast of heat hit his bare toes.

She'd been kidnapped at five years old and, if news reports could be believed, she'd lived a pretty sheltered life with the Altiers. What had her life been like since she'd returned home to Chicago? Had her real family smothered her, too, afraid to let her out of their sight again? Had she ever ventured out on her own before this?

Resisting the urge to glance at her again, he yanked off the rest of his clothes, shivering as the hot air hit his wet skin. There wasn't much space in the passenger seat, but he managed to get the itchy wool blanket wrapped all the way around him. Then he closed his eyes and let the warmth inside the truck seep into him.

Alanna was on his bad ear's side, but in the close confines of the truck, it didn't matter. All too easily, he could hear her moving around, presumably still in the process of undressing. He squeezed his eyes more tightly shut, suddenly picturing the paleness of her skin, the long, lean legs that had been encased in jeans earlier. Things he had no business imagining.

When the noise finally stopped, he asked tightly, "You covered?"

"Yes."

He opened his eyes, trying not to actually glance at her. But he couldn't help himself.

She was wrapped tightly in the dark wool blanket, covered up to her chin with her drenched hair draped over the front of the blanket and sticking to the seat behind her. Her cheeks were still a patchy red, but it was the bright red of standing outside in Alaska too long, not from embarrassment or shyness.

"You okay?" he asked, staring into her deep brown eyes. It suddenly hit him how beautiful she was.

He hadn't noticed it before, not really. He'd been far too busy trying to figure out how she'd gone from kidnap victim to accomplice, enabler and defender of criminals.

But she wasn't out here, risking her life, just for Darcy. She was here for those kids, too, kids she probably identified with because she'd once been in exactly their position. She had to be.

One of her hands slipped free from the mounds of wool and squeezed his arm. "Thank you for coming after me."

"It's lucky I happened to be following you around." As soon as the words were out of his mouth, he regretted them, but she laughed.

"Yeah, I guess so."

"Did you mean what you said earlier? About working together to find those kids?"

Tiny lines appeared between her graceful eyebrows. "Of course."

He leaned closer to her, glancing at the gas gauge, and relaxed when he saw that they still had plenty in the tank. They could sit here and warm up a little bit longer. Then again…

He leaned over her, angling so he was looking upward out the window. Being parked around the bend from where the avalanche had hit was a safer spot. The mountain above didn't come down at quite the same sharp angle. It was less prone to avalanches. Still, if the snow above was unstable, he didn't want to sit here and discover he was wrong.

Alanna had squeezed against the back of her seat and he could practically feel her holding her breath until he sat back and put some distance between them.

"We should probably move."

She twisted in her seat, giving him a glance of bare shoulder as she smiled at Chance, who'd shaken free of the blanket and lay down on the back seat, looking far more relaxed than he should have after digging them out of an avalanche.

"You okay, Chance?"

Her dog lifted his big head, strained forward and licked her cheek.

"Guess so," she said, laughing as she turned forward again. She squirmed inside the blanket until she had it wrapped around her more like a towel, her arms and shoulders bare. Then she twisted and tucked it around her knees and gripped the wheel. "I'm not running around the truck to change seats and I think climbing over each other will be a disaster. So, how about I drive?"

He blinked back at her, suddenly conjuring an image of the two of them tangled together, wool blankets awkwardly between them and nothing else. "You drive and I'll direct. Let's go to my house and figure out a plan."

She stared at him a long minute, the air suddenly tense between them, until finally she gave a short nod and shifted the truck into Drive. She made a careful turn and they headed back up the mountain, past the

Altiers' old home, and then downward again, back to Desparre's downtown.

With every mile, he snuck glances at her, her hands tense on the wheel, her hair slowly drying and curling slightly against the wool blanket. She seemed more serious in profile, older somehow, and Peter wondered which Alanna was the real one.

The woman who'd held tight to her dog, even at the risk of being tossed over the edge of the mountain by the avalanche? Who'd offered to help the police catch someone she obviously still cared about? Who'd blushed when he stripped his sweater off, even when she should have been more concerned about her own physical well-being?

Or was she the person who'd defended the couple who'd kidnapped her? Still the child who'd been molded by two kidnappers, who'd had her emotions manipulated for so long that her loyalty would always lie in the wrong place?

By keeping her close, he could keep her safe. But would he just be putting himself back in the same position he had two years ago, risking his own safety for someone who was beyond saving?

ALANNA MORGAN LOOKED good in his house, looked good in his clothes.

Peter scowled at the ridiculous thought as he handed her a steaming cup of coffee and settled on the chair across from her, Chance on the floor between them. He'd started a fire as soon as they'd walked through the door. Now it was blazing, almost too hot, but it felt good after being buried in the snow. He took a long sip of his coffee, making a mental note to grab their clothes from his truck soon and toss them all in the dryer. The sooner she was back in her own clothes, the better it would be for his focus.

He still had his suspicions about Alanna, still wondered how much he could trust her, but now sympathy was mixed in with those other emotions. She had to be carrying so many conflicting feelings about her past, about Darcy, about her future. He knew that territory well, and he wanted to reassure her that she could make it through just as he had done.

The drive to his house had been quiet. All of Alanna's attention had been on navigating the Alaskan roads and she'd handled them better than most of the locals. It reminded him of something else he'd heard through the rumor mill: the Altiers had taught the kids they'd kidnapped all kinds of survival skills. He knew she could lose a tail better than most police officers. Still, when it came to searching for Darcy, she'd acted with emotion rather than intellect. Both he and Alanna should have known those back mountain roads could be dangerous, and still, they'd persisted.

Was it a mistake to bring her here? A mistake to let her get too close? Because even though she might help him find Darcy and those kids, Alanna was still a threat, too. Maybe not intentionally, but when it came right down to it, who would she choose to help? Those kids and a police officer she'd just met, or a woman who'd raised her for most of her life?

Right now she was glancing around his home with

open curiosity. It was cozy in a definably Alaskan way, with big windows that showcased the wilderness outside, exposed wooden beams and huge, open living spaces. She took in the long row of black-and-white photographs on one wall. They were images from his time overseas, mostly inside war zones. Images his family always complained about when they came over, images they'd pushed him to take down as his nieces and nephews started asking about them. Images he still kept up so he'd never forget. There was only one photo he'd never hung, one that had appeared in newspapers across the country. He touched his bad ear, scowled when he realized what he was doing and refocused on Alanna.

She frowned slightly at the photos, then turned her gaze out the window as he studied her.

Five years ago, he'd been too caught up in his own life to pay a lot of attention to a group of kids, ages six to twenty-three, rescued from kidnappers so near his hometown. But when he'd first come home, feeling totally adrift and with no idea what he'd do with the rest of his life, he'd read a lot about the story. He'd scoffed at statements made by the victims saying they'd been loved and well-treated. But admittedly, he'd been biased by his own experiences. He still was.

"Tell me about life with the Altiers."

She shifted to face him, her suspicion of his motives all over her face. Still, she answered softly, earnestly, "I don't know why she's doing this, but Darcy would never hurt those kids."

"She already has," Peter snapped, regretting the words as he spoke them but unable to call them back.

"She kidnapped them. Don't you remember how that felt?" Way to get beyond his own biases. "I'm sorry." He sighed, not wanting to tell her about his own past but wondering if that was the best way to reach her.

Before he could, she set down her coffee and leaned toward him. Chance's head popped up, glancing between them, obviously sensing the tension. "I do remember. I still have nightmares about it sometimes. I know you don't understand how I can—" she took an audible breath, then stared him straight in the eyes as she finished "—love them."

"I do understand that." Or at least, he understood that she *thought* what she felt was love, instead of a complicated mix of fear and dependency, multiplied over fourteen years. "The attachment you can develop for someone who holds you against your will is real. It can be necessary for survival and then it gets ingrained. It's—"

Her snort of disbelief cut him off. She looked offended when she replied, "I got a psychology degree after I left Alaska. I understand why you think that's what's happening here, but don't forget—I'm the one who turned them in. They both went to jail because I left that note. My... Julian *died* because of me."

Peter frowned, scooting to the edge of his seat, wanting to reach for her hand across the coffee table and assure her that none of it was her fault. But he'd done that once before in his life as a war reporter, and it was amazing he'd come out of that situation with only lost hearing.

She squeezed her eyes briefly shut, then continued,

"I know what they did was wrong. I think *they* know what they did was wrong. But I lived almost my whole childhood with that family. They were the ones who held me when I cried, who made me laugh with their silly jokes, who cheered for me when I accomplished something. The only thing they ever did to hurt me was take me from my family."

"Isn't that enough?" Peter asked, straining to keep his voice neutral.

"That's how my family feels," Alanna said, her hands clasping together so tightly that her knuckles went white. "But how much do you remember from before you were five? If you'd gone to live with someone else for most of your childhood, how many memories would you have of your family before that?"

Probably sensing her distress, Chance stood and went to her, plopping his big head in her lap and making a brief smile spread across her lips. It faded as soon as Peter spoke.

"You're telling me you hardly remembered your family?" He tried to imagine that, being ripped from his family as a kindergartener by two people who then called themselves his parents, who treated him well and raised him with love. An ache twisted in his heart at the idea. Worse, he could suddenly picture it, could understand why she'd grown to love them and probably forgot more and more of life with her real family as the years went on.

"I remembered enough," Alanna answered, her voice softer now, as if she knew she was getting through to him. "But sometimes, love is irrational. And sometimes years of good actions start to outweigh one bad one, no matter how terrible that moment was."

"And still, you turned them in. Why?" What had changed after fourteen years to make her write that note?

"I didn't want to go the rest of my life without ever knowing the parents I vaguely remembered, the sister and brother I'd had."

Something passed over her face, a wave of sadness that told him she'd sacrificed a lot to fulfill that wish. More than just the loss of two people who'd acted like her parents most of her childhood, but also four other kids she'd loved as siblings. Four other kids who, from all accounts, had also felt loved in that household. Who probably missed Alanna as much as she missed them.

"Have you seen Darcy and Julian since they went to jail?"

She stiffened, straightened in a way that made his internal lie detector go off.

"No."

"But you've talked to them?" he guessed.

"No."

Was she lying? He couldn't tell. But if she wasn't... "Alanna, you need to be careful. I know Darcy and Julian loved you once. But you did turn them in. You said what Darcy's doing now makes no sense. Maybe she changed in prison."

He frowned, knowing that in terms of the investigation, it was a mistake to say any more, but he needed her to recognize the threat against her, to keep herself safe, too. She'd agreed to work with him, but theirs was a tentative truce, at best. She didn't trust him any more than he trusted her, even if he was beginning to sympathize with her. Even if he was starting to like her as a person.

That was a mistake, too, but one he couldn't seem to help. These days, it was his job to risk his life to protect others, even if they put him in danger.

He touched his bad ear again, watched her gaze narrow as she followed his movement.

"Darcy would never hurt me," Alanna said, but her voice lacked confidence.

"You can't know that," Peter insisted. "So, let's make a deal. You want to work together to find those kids? I'm in. But I'm law enforcement, so you're going to let me keep you safe. No more going off on your own to search for her. We stick together from here on out. Deal?"

She looked ready to argue, but after a long moment, she simply nodded.

"Now, where were you going today?"

"I think I have some ideas about where Darcy might go. Julian had backup hiding spots."

Anger flooded through him at the realization that she'd kept this to herself. She'd been gunning for one of those hiding spots and if he hadn't been following her, that information would have been lost. Those kids might have been lost. Maybe for fourteen long years, like she had been. Maybe longer.

This time, he held his anger inside and asked, "Where are these hiding spots?"

Panic rushed over her face and she leaped to her feet, making Chance jump up, too. The pair of them ran to his garage, and Alanna yanked open the back door of his truck, climbing inside as he caught up to them.

When Chance tried to climb in with her, Alanna put up a hand. "Stay, Chance."

The St. Bernard promptly sat, but he looked back at Peter as if to say, *Can't I go, too?*

"We're not going anywhere, Chance," Peter told him as Alanna climbed back out, unzipping an interior pocket of her bright red coat.

The coat was still sopping wet and so was the small piece of paper she pulled out of the pocket.

She unfolded it with infinite care, then swore as she looked back up at him, dismay in her eyes. "It's gone."

"What's gone?"

"The list of locations I found at the house. All the places Darcy might be hiding."

Chapter Seven

"I can't believe it's gone," Alanna said, staring at the little scrap of paper. She hadn't been able to toss it in the trash, even after putting it under a blow-dryer confirmed that all the pencil marks were lost.

Peter sat next to her, taking the smaller spot on the couch to her left instead of the bigger space to her right. "You read the list, right? Maybe if you think about it, you can recall some of the places?"

The heat from his body warmed her still-cold legs and she tried not to fixate on his closeness. It was just residual embarrassment from stripping out of her clothes in his car. Even covered by a blanket, it had been awkward. She'd had to use a lot of willpower not to glance his way as he'd stripped off his clothes—thank goodness he'd eventually wrapped a blanket around himself.

The memory made her hyperaware of the shocking blue of his eyes, the sharp lines of his face and the lean power of his build. He wasn't traditionally handsome, but there was something compelling about him. Maybe it was part of what had made him a good war reporter, the ability to project such intensity that it made it hard to look away.

"Alanna?" Peter pressed.

"I read the list. But it was coordinates, latitude and longitude, and it was in code."

"Code? Are you serious?"

"A silly code. My sis—the other kids and I made it up one winter when we had a bad storm and we were stuck inside. It was just a game, but we left codes for each other all over the house for a week." She shrugged at the interest in his gaze, remembering how much fun they'd had running around the house to find coded clues like a scavenger hunt. "My par—the Altiers got in on the game, too. I'd forgotten all about it until I saw this list."

"It sounds like a good time."

His tone was hesitant, speculative, and Alanna held in a sigh. Reporters—at least reporters actively chasing a story—got right to the point. But once anyone else would realize her history, they'd just pick at the edges. They'd ask sideways questions, looking for insight and pretending to understand, before they announced, "But these people *kidnapped* you." As if she didn't know.

Usually, for Alanna, that was the beginning of the end. It was too awkward to try to convince people that she'd been loved, that she'd loved in return. More awkward still to feel like she had to justify it. It was easier to break ties, keep to herself.

When she'd gone back to Chicago, she'd ventured outside her comfort zone with school and volunteer work. But after an initial burst of interest by anyone with the remotest connection to the Morgans, she'd found herself becoming more and more isolated socially. Kensie and Colter, Alanna's new brother-in-law, had decided something had to be done. Alanna had connected with Colter's dog, Rebel, a former Marine Combat Tracker Dog who had been as good for Alanna's anxiety as Colter's PTSD. So they'd found her a dog of her own, rescuing Chance to give to her.

She smiled at the St. Bernard who'd been so little two years ago, a victim of such cruelty that the vets weren't even sure he would survive. Now, still small for his breed, he was a total gentle giant. And he'd definitely rescued her as much as she'd rescued him.

At her smile, Chance pushed his way between the couch and the coffee table to drop his head in her lap. She stroked his head as she told Peter, "Drew and Valerie, the youngest kids, didn't remember their real families at all. They had no idea they were kidnapped. And we—Johnny, Sydney, and I—didn't tell them because they were so young and because honestly, we hardly remembered our own families. How do you break that to someone? Especially when they're happy?"

"Sydney was the one who remembered her family best, right? She was a few years younger than you?"

Alanna eyed him. "You've done your research."

He flinched, actually looking a little ashamed. "I read up on it when I came back home—to what used to be my home—two years ago. I lived on the other side of the mountain, in Luna, where you were reunited with your sister. When you showed up in Desparre this week…"

"You read through all the news reports again?"

He nodded, not quite meeting her gaze.

The coverage in Desparre hadn't been the most flattering, especially after time went on and reporters looked for a new angle to keep the story alive. They'd all seen her as that new angle. She might have turned the Altiers in, but the real story was how she *hadn't* spoken up for fourteen years.

"No wonder you acted like you already knew and disliked me as soon as you heard my name."

The Morgans had tried to keep the negative coverage from her at first. She'd been getting her GED and applying to college then, trying to get out into the world and reenter her life from fourteen years earlier. But she hadn't been able to stop herself from seeking out the news coverage on herself and the rest of the "family" she'd left behind.

"Hey." Peter's voice was soft, his eyebrows lowered as he put his hand over her free one.

She froze, her other hand stalling in Chance's fur, as his long fingers threaded through hers. The unexpected contact made her skin tingle.

"I didn't dislike you as soon as I knew who you were. I just—"

"Distrusted me?"

"Yes."

She hadn't expected him to admit it. Even though she'd already known it was true, the quiet word seemed to leave a physical mark on her chest. She slid her hand free and glanced away, hoping he hadn't seen that he'd hurt her.

She looked back just as quickly, tired of having to explain herself, tired of being judged by what people read in newspapers about her past instead of by who she was or her actions now. "Everyone thinks they would have gotten help right away, that they would have spent all those years hating the people who'd raised them. But if you haven't lived it—"

"I'm not judging you."

"No?"

Chance lifted his head from her lap at her sarcastic tone.

"Do you know why my fa...Julian was killed in jail?"

Peter frowned, gave a brief shake of his head.

"He was protecting a twenty-year-old kid who was being preyed on sexually. The predator stabbed Julian in the chest sixteen times for it." She choked on the last words, imagining the man who'd raised her being cornered, brutally attacked and dying on a filthy prison floor.

Peter reached for her and his intent to pull her into a hug was as clear as the confusion in his eyes. He was struggling to reconcile his idea of a child kidnapper with a man who'd risk his life to protect someone he barely knew.

She blocked his hug with a hand to his chest, resisting the urge to fist her hand into his sweatshirt and yank him toward her. To accept his hug along with the friendship he offered. Friendship she still couldn't tell was real or fake.

Standing, she swallowed back the tears that threatened every time she thought about the report the prison had issued. "I think I should go."

He stood, too, but slowly, caution in his expression. "I'm sorry. You're right. I have no idea what your life was like. All I know about the Altiers is what I've read in the papers or a law enforcement bulletin. I know better than anyone how those things can spin a story. But I spent years in war zones and I also know this— no one is one hundred percent good or bad. Everyone lives in gray areas, making right decisions one day and wrong ones the next. Sometimes the way we think of people is based on what side of the line the majority of those decisions lie. Sometimes, it's based on a single, dramatic incident."

His hand twitched upward, the way she'd seen it do before, and she had a sudden realization. He had his own single, dramatic incident. "What happened?"

He stared at her a long moment, not even pretending to misunderstand, before he nodded and sank back onto the couch.

Chance moved his head to Peter's leg, offering his quiet support in a way Alanna had seen him do hundreds of times at the nonprofit where she worked. From the very beginning, when she'd had him certified as a therapy dog so she could bring him to work with her, he'd had a sense of who needed him most.

"I was a war reporter," Peter said, and she nodded, having seen his bylines a time or two. Mostly, she remembered his name from an incident a few years ago, with a picture that had made national headlines: Peter, less fit than he was now, wearing a helmet and covered in sand and blood, one hand to his ear and an expression of horror and disbelief etched on his face.

"You were covering some kind of hostage release," she said, realizing that must have been the incident.

"It was supposed to be smooth and simple. I'd been in far more dangerous situations. The military had brought the ransom money. We were just tagging along—my camera guy and me—to catch the exchange. The hostage-takers hadn't covered their faces—they didn't think they could be identified or they didn't care. The CIA sent one of their officers to make the exchange. She was supposed to walk halfway and leave the money. Then the hostage would walk to us and the hostage-takers would pick up the money and leave. Well, they did take the money and leave."

Peter's hand went halfway to his left ear, then he set it on Chance's head instead, slowly petting the big dog.

"The hostage had been captive for almost six months. She'd watched the other two people who'd been kidnapped with her get killed. We thought she'd be running toward us. But the closer she got, I could see…"

He trailed off, his brows furrowed and his gaze on the wall of photographs across the room.

"What?" Alanna prompted softly.

"I've been to a few hostage exchanges before, where they're expected to go smoothly and our country wants a little good press. Sometimes, the hostages look terrified that something is going to go wrong at any second and they'll be yanked back into the hell they'd been living. Other times, they're crying with relief that it's finally over. And occasionally, they seem like they're not even aware of what's happening. Not this hostage. She was…calm, focused. Stoic, even."

His hand stalled on Chance's head and Alanna set her hand carefully on top of his, offering silent support the way he had for her. The same way she might at work with a survivor or a family member she'd gotten to know over months of visits.

He met her gaze briefly, a hint of a smile twitching on the edge of his lips. Then he looked back at his photos. "I was standing closest when the explosion went off."

Even though she'd seen the photos, had known he'd been close to an explosion, she still gasped at the idea of him being nearest to a bomb. Her fingers clenched reflexively over his. Chance's head tipped up, his attention bouncing to her, then back to Peter.

Alanna tried to remember the details of the article she'd read two years ago, but all she could recall were the details of the photo. Of Peter's face, dripping with blood. Back then, it had been a horrible sight, but now, knowing Peter made every detail more painful. She felt an ache in her chest thinking about what he'd experienced. "What happened? The hostage-takers threw a bomb during the rescue?"

He gave a humorless laugh, his gaze focused on her once more, all his intensity and cynicism directed at her. "They didn't throw anything. It was strapped to the hostage. She set it off herself when she got close to us."

Tension bloomed between them as she stared back at him. Suddenly, it all made sense. His instant distrust of her, his insistence that she must be working with Darcy. He thought she was just like the hostage who'd almost killed him: willing to do whatever it took to help someone she should have wanted behind bars, at the expense of anyone else. As that realization dawned, Peter said softly, "I quit my job after that. I'd wanted to be a reporter my whole life, but after that moment, I never wanted to go into another war zone. I sat around for a good six months, then saw a job posting for a police officer. This hostage almost destroyed that dream, too. The police have strict fitness and health requirements, and with the extent of my hearing loss... They only took me because they were desperate for officers."

His hand went up again, and this time, he did touch his left ear. "I lost most of the hearing in this ear in the explosion."

Alanna's heart gave a sudden, painful ache. He thought she was the same as that woman who, in the face of rescue, had destroyed herself and tried to take out everyone around her in the process. No wonder Peter didn't trust her.

He was never going to trust her.

ALANNA WAS SILENT in the passenger seat as Peter drove her and Chance in his truck the long way around the base of the mountain the next day. They were headed for Luna. Five years ago, Luna police had stopped the Altiers and arrested them. They'd loaded her and her "siblings" into a police car and driven them to the Luna hospital to be checked out. It was the last place she'd seen any of the people she'd called family for most of her childhood.

Last night, Peter had asked if she wanted to go there, to get checked out at the hospital after being trapped in that avalanche. But she had no desire to go back to that hospital, to those memories. And besides still feeling cold and being exhausted, she'd been okay. The worst of it was calling her rental company to let them know what had happened to their truck.

The fastest way to get to Luna was actually to drive up into the mountain and then back down. But after the avalanche yesterday, that wasn't happening. So, she and Peter had spent an awkward hour and a half in his truck. They had at least another hour to go before they made it to the far side of town, where Alanna thought one of Julian's hideouts might be.

She'd spent a long time last night trying to decode the old cipher she and her "siblings" had created, without much luck. But in the morning, she'd had an epiphany about one of them. Hopefully, she was right, because she'd convinced Peter to trust her and come along without notifying his department.

There was a new tension between them since he'd admitted what had happened to him. The uncomfortable silence was worse than sleeping in Peter's guest bedroom, hearing him move around one room over. Smelling like his soap and shampoo, and knowing he hadn't insisted she stay at his place because of the roads, like he'd claimed. The truth was, he didn't trust her not to go off on her own, even though she'd promised she wouldn't.

She squeezed her hands tightly together and said, "Maybe that woman didn't blow herself up. Maybe the explosive had a remote detonator."

"No," Peter replied, not even sounding surprised to

hear the suggestion after an hour and a half of near-silence. "There was an investigation. She set it off herself."

"Well, you don't know what they told her. Maybe she felt like she had no choice. Maybe they threatened to kill her family if she didn't do it. I've heard that more than once from victims of violent crime. The person who did it threatens someone they love if they ever talk. After the things they've suffered, the victim believes it. This could be a more extreme version."

"Maybe," Peter agreed. He glanced her way, looking intrigued, and she realized that he didn't know what she did for a living.

"I work for a nonprofit back home." Calling anywhere *home* besides Desparre still felt strange, especially now that she was back in Alaska, but it was true. Chicago had become her home now.

The thought wiggled around in her brain, bittersweet. Maybe she was truly starting to let go of the people she'd loved most of her life.

Her parents, Kensie, Colter and Flynn had all worked hard to bring her into their lives, to show her how much they loved her. There was still so much missing, so many memories with them she'd never be able to have, but she'd never stopped loving them, either.

Shaking off her musings for another time, Alanna said, "The nonprofit works with victims of violent crime."

"You're a therapist?" He sounded surprised.

"No. It's not that kind of place. We do have support groups, and I've gotten Chance certified as a therapy dog so he can come and sit with people. But we also help people navigate the legal system, act as an intermediary with police when necessary and help them transition back to their regular life. Technically, my job is as a case manager, so I help identify what people need when they first come to us."

"Why did you choose violent crime?"

She darted a glance at him, expecting to see suspicion on his face. When most people heard about her past and her career choice, they assumed she'd been harmed during her years with the Altiers, despite her insistence otherwise.

"I guess I just…" She sighed, wishing it was something she knew how to put in words. "When I came home, I got a lot of attention. All these people I didn't know wanted to help me. They meant well, even if it made me anxious to have them come up to me and ask for details, looking like they just wanted a good story. But in some ways, it was a good thing. The fact that we were all found after so many years inspired a pair of ex-cops who lived near me to start a cold case club. They've solved a dozen cases since then."

Peter nodded, his gaze catching hers briefly before he looked back out the front windshield. The road had been cleared yesterday, but had a new dusting of snow from the morning. "You're doing it out of guilt."

She frowned. "Not guilt—"

"I don't mean it in a bad way. Just—I get it. You feel like these other people who had it worse than you should be getting the attention, the resources, you did."

"Sort of." She fidgeted in her seat, uncomfortable

sharing this but somehow feeling he'd empathize. No one else had understood it quite so well. "I also understand how confusing it is to try to fit back into your normal life. I don't identify with the way most of these people have been harmed. But I understand some of it. My case got a lot of press, so most of them recognize my name. They tell me it makes them feel more connected to me, because I've personally experienced some of it. And I like helping people."

"You're a good person."

There was such honesty in his voice, mixed with just a hint of surprise, that Alanna wasn't sure what to say. Her "thanks" was delayed and too quiet.

Peter shrugged, giving her a little grin that sent a flutter of awareness through her. "Don't thank me. That's all on you."

She felt herself grin in response and the tension that had filled the truck since they'd sat together at his breakfast table this morning finally eased. Even Chance seemed to feel it, scooting forward and shoving his head through the space between the seats.

Alanna stroked his silky fur as she stared at Peter's profile. She had a sudden vision of the first moment he'd approached her four days ago, the way he'd angled his body, making his weapon more visible. But his right side wasn't just where he kept his gun; it was also the side with his good ear. He'd done it so he could hear her better, not to intimidate her.

Maybe there were other things she was misinterpreting, too. Yes, he'd admitted he hadn't trusted her when he'd met her. But he'd let her stay in his house.

He'd called in to work this morning and she'd overheard him telling someone he was running a lead today and would be late for his Sunday shift. He hadn't mentioned her involvement.

It was the deal they'd struck. She'd share the location she thought she'd figured out from the ruined list and they'd check it out, just the two of them.

So far, he was keeping up his end of the bargain. She had her doubts that he would continue to do so if they actually found Darcy, but this seemed to be the best way forward.

She'd insisted on secrecy because she'd feared if police showed up, it would escalate everything and Darcy might do something stupid. Alanna's gut clenched at the memory of Darcy and Johnny shooting at Kensie five years ago. If the police were there this time, they would see the kidnapper lifting a weapon as a legitimate reason to open fire in return. Her concern had been that Darcy would end up getting herself killed.

But suddenly, she was struck with a totally different worry.

If it was just her and Darcy, Alanna wanted to believe she could talk some sense into the woman who'd raised her since she was five years old. She wanted to believe that if Peter's presence threatened Darcy, Alanna standing in front of him would keep him safe. But was that realistic?

Or was she fooling herself?

As Peter met her gaze again, giving her a quick, genuine smile, she tried to smile back.

He was prickly, and she still wasn't totally sure where

she stood with him. But he was smart and capable and he'd run to save her when he could have just as easily stepped back and saved himself from that avalanche. From the moment he'd wrapped his fingers in her coat and held on even as the snow threatened to send them both over a mountain, she'd started to care about him. Probably more than she should.

If she was wrong about Darcy, was she risking Peter's life by bringing him with her?

Chapter Eight

Peter stared at Alanna across the tiny wooden table in the overcrowded coffee shop in downtown Luna. She was back in the jeans and light purple sweater she'd been wearing yesterday, but he couldn't stop picturing her the way she'd looked last night in his too-large sweatpants and long-sleeved T-shirt.

She flushed at his stare, redirecting her gaze to the steaming cup of coffee in her hands. At her side, Chance sat patiently, his size making him look like her protector.

The coffee shop had been here since he was a teenager and he'd spent hours in front of the fireplace over the years. Playing board games from the stack the owners always kept on hand or reading a book from the shelves on the far wall. With a first date or a long-term girlfriend. With family or a group of friends. Or, in those first six months after coming home, feeling adrift and unsure of what the rest of his life held, by himself.

They were less than twenty minutes from the location Alanna thought she'd identified from the Altiers' coded list. Peter had told her he wanted to stop here to take a break from driving, to rest a little before a possible confrontation with Darcy. The truth was, he needed to give his fellow officers a chance to catch up.

He'd called in to the station that morning, giving the story he and Alanna had agreed upon: he was running a long-shot lead and would let them know how it panned out. She'd been just around the corner, listening in, not realizing he could see her reflection in the mirror across the hall.

When she'd slipped back down the hall, he'd quickly texted Tate with the real story. He felt guilty about it— and Tate had also reminded him that technically, the Desparre police department had no jurisdiction here. But he trusted his partner. He didn't know the Luna officers. He had no idea what Darcy would do if she was cornered, but he wanted to make sure Alanna was safe.

Still, he didn't like betraying her trust.

A few days ago, that wouldn't have mattered to him. He would have considered it a necessary lie for the possibility of rescuing those kids. Now, after the things she'd shared about her life with the Altiers, he understood why her loyalty was conflicted. For the first time in two years, he even sympathized with the woman who'd killed herself—and almost killed him—when she'd been on the verge of being rescued.

He'd always pitied her. But there'd been too much anger for more than that. Peter had always assumed the hostage had been brainwashed, that she'd hit that detonator to protect the terrorists who had taken her. Maybe he'd been wrong. Maybe she'd done it to protect her family, because after nearly six months of being terrorized, she could see no other option.

"What are you thinking?" Alanna asked.

When he blinked and refocused, he realized she was staring at him with an expression that said too many emotions had been obvious on his face.

"You're nothing like I expected," he blurted. From all the headlines, all the newspaper stories, he'd expected a conflicted, confused woman who'd grown up isolated and brainwashed, who'd come to Desparre for her own agenda.

A hesitant smile turned up her lips, warmed her deep brown eyes. "I assume that's a good thing?"

He was attracted to her. The realization slammed into him with an intensity that made him slump back in his chair. It wasn't just her long, silky hair, those plump lips or the secrets in the depths of her eyes. He'd seen too much as a reporter, on both sides of the camera, to really care about that anymore. It was the integrity of her character, the way she tried to do right by everyone, whether they deserved it or not. It was the way she'd clung to Chance in that avalanche, even when letting him go might have been safer for her. It was the way she challenged Peter at every turn, made him rethink his assumptions about everything.

"What?" she asked, sounding concerned as she leaned toward him, put her hand over his.

"Peter!"

What terrible timing. Peter slowly swiveled in his chair to find his parents standing behind him, both holding takeout cups of coffee. His father was looking at

Alanna curiously. His mother was smiling at him in a way that told him she'd totally misunderstood what was happening.

"Mom, Dad." He stood, hugged them both and then gestured to Alanna, who was also standing. "This is Alanna."

When Chance gave a short bark, attracting attention from nearby customers, Peter laughed and added, "And this big guy is Chance."

The St. Bernard wagged his tail at the introduction and Peter's mom scratched his ears as his dad shook Alanna's hand.

"Do you live in Luna, Alanna?" his mom asked, giving him a quick grin she probably thought was subtle.

He wanted to laugh and roll his eyes at the same time. Getting him to move back to Luna was a dream she was unwilling to give up on, even now that he'd lived and worked in Desparre for a year.

"Actually, I live in Chicago."

His mom's brow furrowed, then she breathed, "You're Alanna Morgan, aren't you?" Before Alanna could answer, she looked at Peter with concern in her eyes. "This isn't another story, is it?"

"No, Mom." He shook his head at Alanna for emphasis, but she didn't seem worried by the question, just uncomfortable that his mom had recognized her.

His mom seemed to realize it, too, because she smiled again and said, "Well, we're just off to a movie. You two have a nice time."

"Come by for dinner soon," his dad said as they headed for the door.

"They're nice," Alanna said.

"They're still upset I've moved to Desparre. They thought when I finally gave up being a reporter, I'd come home to Luna like my brothers and sister."

She leaned toward him. "You've got siblings?"

Peter glanced at the front of the shop and saw his mom grinning back at him before she slipped out the door. He realized that she might have incorrectly thought this was a date, but in some ways, it felt like one.

"Three," he replied, shifting his full attention back to Alanna, suddenly wishing they could both shake free of their past baggage, of their reasons for being here together right now. Wishing it was really a date. But he could pretend it was, if only for a few minutes, to buy time. "Two older brothers and one older sister. They've all got kids and they all live in Luna. My parents keep hoping I'll follow their lead."

Alanna smiled, sipping her coffee. "That's nice."

He shrugged. "It's a nice idea." But he'd always been restless, always wanted to get out and see the world, do something that got his blood moving, that made a difference. For five years, he'd done it as a reporter. Since he'd returned to Alaska, he'd discovered that being a police officer filled that need. He'd never been able to understand how the rest of his family didn't have the same restlessness.

"You wouldn't ever move back to Luna?"

"Probably not. Don't get me wrong—I love my family. But it's not like there are tons of opportunities in Luna. They're lucky I got the police officer spot nearby."

"Well, it's close until Desparre gets a particularly bad snow and you can't get over here for months," she said, reminding him that she knew Desparre at least as well as he did.

"When I was a reporter, sometimes they wouldn't see me for six months at a time."

"It's got to be hard for them. First, you're in war zones and now you're a police officer, potentially under fire at any given moment." She looked a little queasy at the idea.

"My grandparents moved here from Czechoslovakia—back when that's what it was called. During the Czech uprising in 1968, when the Soviets sent in half a million tanks and troops, they fled. At first, they thought they'd stick around, be part of the protests. But they didn't like living among so many tanks, the constant unspoken threat of violence. Ultimately they decided they had to get out—about three hundred thousand people there felt the same way. My grandparents said they came here because they just wanted to be left alone. I grew up hearing their stories and the stories they'd been told by *their* parents about what their country was like at the time of the Nazi invasion."

Alanna nodded slowly, probably thrown by his change of topic. "I don't blame them for wanting to live peacefully, quietly, after all of that."

"Yeah, I guess," Peter said. His parents had wanted the same thing and so did his siblings. "But I always felt like it was in my blood to get out there and witness conflict. To record it for history and, hopefully, help prevent us from repeating it." He shrugged, suddenly embarrassed by how naive he sounded.

She reached across the table and put her hand on his. "I understand that, too."

She understood because in her own way, she'd chosen a similar path. They were both in professions to help others.

He smiled back at her, realizing how natural it felt to be sitting in this coffee shop with her, their hands stacked together. If this *had* been a date, if she was someone he'd met who lived in Desparre or Luna, he'd already be planning to ask her out again.

His smile faded. If she was right, if they found Darcy hiding in Luna, it would all be over. Alanna would return home and he'd never see her again.

FROM THE MOMENT they'd set foot in Alaska, Darcy and Julian had loved the mountains. So Alanna wasn't surprised when Peter slowed the truck near the location she'd identified and it was at the base of the mountain they'd driven on last night.

When they'd settled in Desparre, Darcy and Julian had built their home at the edge of the mountaintop, with the natural protection of a steep slope at their back. Here, apparently, they'd done the same thing in reverse. Only this time, there was just Darcy.

The cabin was much smaller than the one in Desparre. It looked like a single-room shack and if anyone drove close enough to see it through the trees, it seemed deserted.

Alanna's shoulders dropped as she peered through

the windshield. "What if I'm wrong?" There had been four other locations on that list, but although she'd tried to recall the other symbols and decode them, nothing she'd worked out in the little notebook Peter had given her made sense yet. She wasn't sure it ever would.

Peter's hands were resting lightly on the wheel, but there was an excitement in his gaze that told her how much he loved chasing leads. "What's the likelihood that there'd be a cabin at the exact longitude and latitude you decoded?"

He was right about that. Like a lot of Alaska, the towns of Desparre and Luna were more open land than homes or businesses. Her discouragement turned to anxiety. "Maybe I should go up to the door alone. If she's there, I might be able to talk her into giving herself up."

"We agreed we'd go together," Peter replied, then turned into the driveway.

"If she's here, you're going to scare her o—"

The words died on her lips as the cabin's front door opened and Darcy stepped halfway through the threshold, backlit by a light inside that had been blocked by the heavy curtains on the windows.

Shock jolted through Alanna. She'd come all the way to Alaska to find Darcy, but after five years, on some level, she'd never expected to see her again. All the letters Darcy and Julian had sent from prison had gone unanswered, mostly because Alanna knew how much it would hurt her biological parents for her to respond, how badly they needed her to make a clean break. She couldn't bring herself to cut off her "siblings," so she'd made the choice to cut off Darcy and Julian. Every letter had been returned, unopened.

All these years later, it still physically hurt to wonder what Darcy and Julian had written her. Had they been letters of remorse, letters of love? Or had their love turned to hate over the note she had written and left in Jasper's General Store in an attempt to go home to the Morgans?

Darcy had been sentenced to sixty-two years in prison without the possibility of parole. Julian had gotten sixty-three years, and if he hadn't been killed in prison, he would still have died there. Since the moment she'd chosen not to communicate with them, Alanna had hardened herself to the idea of never seeing Darcy or Julian again. In so many ways, it had felt like the right thing to do, the only thing she *could* do. A penance she had to make for fourteen years of silence.

The Darcy in front of her was thinner, her hair almost entirely gray and lackluster. Her once stick-straight posture was now slumped, defeated. Every day she'd spent in prison seemed to show in the new lines on her face.

Alanna couldn't take her gaze off Darcy as she climbed out of Peter's truck and took a step up the driveway. Behind her, she heard Chance leap over the seat and out the door.

Across the thirty feet separating them, Darcy's eyes seemed to widen comically, then her gaze darted right. Toward Peter. Her eyes narrowed, her lips twisting into an angry scowl. When she stepped fully outside, there was a pistol tucked into her belt at her hip and a shotgun clutched in her hand.

It was a nightmare right out of her memory. Five years seemed to disappear, and instead of Peter beside her, it was Kensie, who had found her after so many years lost. She could see Darcy lifting that shotgun and firing at the truck where Kensie and Colter sat. Alanna heard the echoes of her own screams from back then in her ears as she threw her hands wide and ran toward Darcy.

This time, although Darcy's gaze kept darting toward Peter—and then toward the street, like she expected backup to come flying in, sirens blaring, at any second—she never lifted her gun. Instead, as Alanna got closer, slowing to a walk until she stood still a few feet away, Darcy shook her head and whispered, "*Why?*"

Up close, the lines on Darcy's face were even more pronounced, the dark circles under her eyes more hollow. Anger lurked just underneath the hurt that flashed in her eyes. The pain and betrayal she felt were as obvious in her voice as the tears she was trying to blink back. "*Why?*" she demanded again, this time almost a scream.

Chance stepped up beside Alanna and she reached for him fast, put a steadying hand on his head to assure him she wasn't in danger.

Darcy's gaze shifted to Chance and her lips shifted into a strange semblance of a smile, an echo of what it had once been. Too quickly, it dropped away. "When you were little, you always wanted a dog." She looked back at Alanna, blinking rapidly. "Guess you got everything you wanted."

Then somehow Peter was beside her, his hand gripping her arm too hard, keeping her in place. His other hand was on the butt of his weapon. "We just want the kids. That's it. You hand them over and we walk away."

Darcy did little more than smirk at Peter's offer, her hand shifting on the shotgun with an ease that told Alanna she might look older and weaker, but Darcy still had an unexpected strength. Then her gaze was back on Alanna.

"Who is this? Why is he here?"

"He's my friend, Peter," Alanna said, glad that it was common in Alaska for people to carry weapons. It didn't immediately mark him as law enforcement. "He drove me out here."

"How did you find me?"

"This is where we were headed five years ago, isn't it?" Alanna asked instead of answering.

Darcy's slight nod, as if she couldn't stop herself from responding, was enough to tell Alanna it was true.

Her own anger flared up, the unfairness of it all, the blame she felt from all directions no matter what choices she made. "And then what was the plan? To keep running, go back to what we did when I was little?"

"We wouldn't have needed to do that if you hadn't left that note. We were good to you. We *loved* you." Darcy shook her head, as if she still didn't understand it.

Alanna's gut clenched at Darcy's use of the past tense, but as much as it hurt, this moment wasn't about her. It was about those two kids who had to be in the cabin behind Darcy, probably terrified and confused like Alanna had been in those early days with the Altiers.

"There was another family out there who loved me,

too." On some level, Darcy had to know what she'd done was wrong. Didn't she? "How do you think it felt, knowing I'd never get to see them again?"

Something flashed in Darcy's eyes, some mix of guilt and sorrow that was gone so fast Alanna wondered if she'd imagined it. Then Darcy's attention veered left, into the woods at the base of the mountain. Was that where she'd hidden her vehicle? Was she thinking about making a run for it?

"Please," Alanna whispered. "It's not too late to do the right thing."

A spasm of emotion passed over Darcy's face and for a moment, Alanna thought she'd gotten through to her. Then Darcy swung the shotgun up, past Alanna and Peter, high over the woods to her left.

Alanna's hand darted out to grab Peter, to prevent him from pulling his own weapon. What was Darcy doing? Trying to scare them? Had she lost her mind when she'd lost her "kids"?

The *boom boom boom* of the shotgun firing repeatedly echoed, followed by a louder, heavier rumble that made Alanna's heart seem to drop to her stomach. She recognized that sound, had felt the weight of the snow burying her only yesterday.

Her gaze traveled up the side of the mountain, to the weak spot where Darcy had aimed, an overhang of snow that was now rushing downward. It was far enough away that it was unlikely to reach them, so Peter's scream to *watch out* startled her, made her jump.

Then, suddenly, everything around her was noise and motion.

Peter raced toward the oncoming snow, Chance at his heels, as shapes emerged from behind the trees, people trying to escape the avalanche. People who shouldn't have been there at all. People who weren't moving fast enough.

Darcy's gaze lingered on Alanna for a drawn-out moment, then she darted the other way, back into the cabin, slamming the door behind her.

Alanna glanced toward Peter and Chance and the police officers who'd been hiding in the woods, who were being overrun by the snow. Then she glanced back at the cabin, where Darcy was hiding with two young children.

And she made her choice.

Chapter Nine

For the second time in two days, Peter was running toward an avalanche.

He'd lived in Alaska for most of his life and managed to never get caught up in one before this past week. Like most people who lived this far north, he had a healthy respect for the power of nature but he'd always taken precautions, so he'd never feared it. The way his heart was thundering in his chest now, that had changed.

This time, he wasn't in any real danger of being buried in it. The snow had already stopped falling from above and the rush through the woods was slowing. That was both good and bad. The trees acting as a natural blockade for some of the snow meant it wouldn't spill over to the cabin, where he assumed those kids were being held. But it also meant more of it was piled higher in the exact location he'd last spotted his fellow officers. Including his partner.

"Tate!" he yelled. Now that the thundering of snow was quieting, his voice echoed along the mountain base, taunting him with the lack of response.

He slowed to a stop before he reached the snow, realizing he should have run to his truck instead to grab the collapsible snow shovel most people who lived in these parts always carried. He spun back even as Chance raced past him, right into the snow.

His call for Alanna to grab his shovel died on his lips. He scanned the area around the cabin. But there were only woods and an empty driveway. She must have followed Darcy inside.

Pain clamped in his chest as he glanced back to the snow, where Chance was frantically digging, then over to the silent cabin. He ran back the way he'd come, heading for his truck and shovel.

He had to pray that Alanna was right and Darcy wouldn't hurt her. He had to pray that Alanna would be able to talk Darcy into handing over the kids without hurting anyone.

There was no mistaking that the woman still loved Alanna like a daughter. It was equally obvious that she felt deeply betrayed and probably blamed Alanna for the years she'd spent in jail, maybe even for her husband's death. Peter could imagine things going shockingly well, that he might turn back and see Alanna ushering out two relieved kids and a sobbing Darcy. Or he might hear a series of shotgun blasts and then Darcy fleeing for safety alone.

Right now he had to trust that Alanna was right. That the love Darcy still felt for her was stronger than the hate. That the education in psychology Alanna had earned and her experience working with vulnerable people would have taught her how to navigate such a volatile situation. One thing he did know: Darcy hadn't fired that shotgun at him before because Alanna had called him her friend. If he burst through that cabin door as an officer, Darcy would shoot.

Alanna had a chance. But his teammates didn't. No way could Chance dig all of them out alone before someone suffocated.

Peter holstered his gun, grabbing his shovel and dialing his phone as he ran. "Chief," he huffed when Chief Hernandez answered, "I need help out here fast. Avalanche." He didn't wait for her response, just tucked his phone back in his pocket and started digging beside Chance.

The big dog had already uncovered the legs of an officer who was facedown. "Good boy, Chance," said Peter. The dog gave a quick bark, then left Peter to finish digging the man out. He bounded a few feet over and started digging again, his big paws sending snow flying, his strong nose right on target as another pair of boots appeared.

"Come on," Peter muttered, trading the shovel for his thinly gloved hands as he got close to the man's face. The fact that he hadn't moved the whole time Peter and Chance had been digging him out was a bad sign, but as Peter swept snow off the back of his head, he suddenly groaned and rolled partway over.

Charlie Quinn was a longtime member of the force, someone Peter had overheard more than once complaining about working with "the pity-hire who can't hear." But when Peter had asked for backup, he'd shown up without complaint.

"You okay?" Peter asked, helping him to a sitting position.

Charlie put a shaky hand to his head, nodding.

"More help is coming," Peter told him, leaving him there so he could go dig out the next officer Chance had found.

As soon as Peter got there, Chance gave him an encouraging *woof* and was off again, sniffing his way to a new spot.

"You're amazing," Peter breathed as he paused a second to watch the St. Bernard. Then he looked back at the partly uncovered officer in front of him and went to work. His hands, arms, and even his face stung as he shoveled snow aside and the cold seeped into him. Finally, he shoved enough snow away to identify the officer.

This wasn't Tate either, but Nate Dreymond. He was the second-newest officer on the force, a twenty-year-old who'd been hired six months before Peter. He was already moving around, flailing and trying to get free of the snow.

"I've got you," Peter said, dropping the shovel and pushing a heavy pile of snow off the young officer, who broke free of the rest covering him so fast and hard that he knocked Peter over.

Nate was gasping, tears and snot mixed with the snow he was raking off his face with bare fingers so pale Peter knew he couldn't feel them.

"Be careful," Peter said, pulling Nate's hands free to reveal he'd scraped up his own face. "Go over there." He pointed toward Charlie. "Help get him into my truck. The heat is on."

As Nate stumbled that way, unsteady on his feet, Peter warned, "There might still be an armed fugitive in the cabin."

Nate didn't show any sign of hearing him, but Charlie looked up sharply, his hand already on the butt of his pistol. He nodded confidently at Peter, pushing to his feet with a grunt. Then the two of them were leaning on each other and moving toward the truck.

Peter spun away from them again, trudging after Chance, the snow up way past the top of his boots now. He was soaked almost to his hips, the cold making him shiver violently. Ignoring it, he took over from Chance's latest dig and the dog was off again, toward an area of snow that was moving, someone clearly fighting to get free.

Yet again, the man Peter finished digging out wasn't Tate. It was Lorenzo Riera, another veteran. As soon as he was freed enough from the snow to speak, he demanded, "Rook?" It was his nickname for Nate, who was his partner.

"He's okay," Peter assured him, glancing over at where Chance was digging away, praying his own partner was under there. How many officers had come to back him up today? How many were hurt right now because of a decision he'd made?

"Peter!"

Peter glanced back as a police SUV screeched to a halt at the edge of the woods, windows down and Chief Hernandez steering one-handed as she leaned partway out the window. The fact that she'd gotten here so fast meant she must have already been out somewhere on the edges of Desparre on a call.

"Status!" she demanded.

"We've got three dug out," Peter called back. "Not sure how many more officers were out here. Presumably Darcy Altier is still in the cabin, armed, with the kids and now Alanna."

The chief was scowling as she slammed the SUV door shut. She had her weapon out of the holster before the door was closed and she nodded at the two officers who stepped out of the back of the vehicle, both in bulletproof vests and helmets.

"Luna police are sending backup. The state police sniper and hostage negotiator are both on another call. We're going to have to breach."

"No!" Peter took two steps toward her, then glanced back at Chance, still digging.

The big dog looked over at him once, let out a long howl, then went back to work.

"Just wait," Peter begged Chief Hernandez. "Give Alanna a chance."

As he pivoted toward Chance and whoever was still buried in the snow, Lorenzo stumbled over next to him to help.

"It's just Tate left. That must be him."

Peter fell to his knees next to Chance, not even bothering to run back for the shovel he'd dropped. He started digging with his hands, shoving snow away from Tate, who'd been moving before but wasn't any longer.

When an arm fell free, Peter tugged on it, trying to

pull Tate out of the snow. His head appeared and while Lorenzo and Chance continued to dig around the rest of him, Peter cleared snow off his face.

Tate looked abnormally pale and his lips had a blu-ish tinge, but when Peter leaned close to listen for his breathing, Tate gasped in a large breath. Lorenzo cleared a big chunk of snow off his back and Peter helped pull Tate to his feet.

"We should have stayed on the road instead of hiding in the woods," Tate choked out, which made Lorenzo let out a relieved laugh.

Peter threw his arms around his friend, hugging him tight. Then he dropped to his knees and hugged Chance. "Good boy," he whispered, and got a big, slobbery kiss on the cheek in return.

Standing, he told Tate, "Now we need to get Alanna out of that cabin safely."

The look on his partner's face—one of dread and sorrow—made him spin to face the cabin.

Sam Jennings and Max Becker—the two officers who'd arrived in vests with the chief—were breach-ing the front door of the cabin, sending it right off the hinges with a powerful blow from a battering ram.

Peter's "*wait!*" was lost beneath the *boom* of the flash-bang tossed through the threshold. As white light exploded behind the curtained windows, the two offi-cers rushed inside.

Even though he knew it was too late, Peter started running. His heart pounded harder than it had for his first raid. Every freezing-cold intake of breath seemed to seize his lungs.

A flash-bang was disorienting—basically a stun grenade that rendered your eyes and ears useless. When used on civilians, they dropped their weapons to cover their eyes or ears. By the time they figured out what was happening, they were being shoved to the ground by tactical officers.

But the Desparre police force rarely used them, and they didn't have a tactical unit. All they had were regular officers who received special tactical and weapons training each month in case an emergency unraveled too quickly to wait for state police or the FBI. Five years in war zones had taught Peter that sometimes it didn't matter what weapons or tactics were used. With a determined-enough opponent, impossible odds suddenly became possible.

He didn't know a lot about Darcy Altier beyond what he'd read and what Alanna had told him. But he'd witnessed her state of mind. She was volatile, desperate, prone to big swings of emotion. And right now she had three hostages who might be between her and the officers who'd rushed inside blind.

Chief Hernandez was moving, arms spread wide, to block him from rushing into the house. Peter paused, unsure whether to race around her or run right through her.

Then Sam and Max emerged from the cabin, looking grim and shaking their heads.

Peter choked on the sudden emotion that rushed up his throat, then he was pushing the chief aside and running into the cabin.

He waved his hands around to clear the smoke, expecting to see all of them—Alanna, Darcy and the two kids—dead on the floor. But there was nothing but an abandoned shotgun on the floor.

He glanced around, wondering if he'd missed another room, but there were no doors except the open one leading out the back. Darcy and the kids were gone.

So was Alanna.

Chapter Ten

"Follow their footsteps," Chief Hernandez ordered, already out in front with her weapon raised.

Peter hurried up beside her, insisting, "We need to be careful. We have to assume Darcy is holding the kids. She dropped the shotgun, but she still has a pistol. Alanna is probably trying to talk her down."

Chief Hernandez gave him a look full of disappointment and disbelief, then motioned for Sam and Max to catch up.

They were tracking two fresh sets of footsteps that led away from the back door of the cabin, with stride distances that indicated the people who made them had been running. The tracks led through the woods in the opposite direction of where the officers had been buried under snow. Back in the direction of downtown Luna. But before that, they would hit a road that might take them toward Desparre or farther north into even more remote parts of the state.

There'd been no vehicle in the driveway, no garage. Had Darcy hidden it at the edge of the woods, near the road, so the cabin would look deserted? That was logical.

Peter put on a burst of speed, panting with exertion that would make his gun hand shake if he caught up to Darcy and she swung her pistol his way. He passed Chief Hernandez, Sam and Max, ignoring his boss's curse and shout to wait. If they hadn't already left, if Alanna was with them, Peter wanted to reach them first.

Darting around trees, Peter's gaze shifted back and forth from the footsteps in the snow to the area in front of him, hoping he wouldn't misjudge a step, run right into a tree and knock himself out. He slowed as the road became visible and then skidded to a stop at its edge, where the footsteps ended and deep tire indents marked the spot where a vehicle had once sat.

They were gone.

A big chunk of snow fell off a tree overhead onto his head, sliding down his face and inside the back of his coat. He wiped it away just as the chief caught up to him.

"This was a total disaster." Holstering her weapon, Chief Hernandez got in his face—not an easy task, since she was a good four inches shorter.

Still, Peter straightened and clamped his jaw shut. He knew better than to piss off the chief—at least any more than he already had.

"When I tell you to wait, you *wait*." She poked a finger at his chest, fury in her gaze. "You're *my* responsibility, Robak. We're not a big police force, but we're a team. If you want to be part of it, you need to act like it."

She strode past him, heading down the road back toward the cabin. Sam and Max followed her. Sam gave him an apologetic glance; Max ignored him entirely.

Peter's shoulders slumped and a shiver racked his body as the cold and exhaustion hit. His jeans and gloves were completely soaked through and the snow that had dripped down the back of his coat was uncomfortable. He looked once more down the road, then followed his fellow officers.

Had Alanna *chosen* to get in that vehicle with Darcy? Or had she been forced inside?

He frowned as he glanced at the ground in front of him. Was that an extra set of footprints he was seeing? Had someone else come back this way? Had Alanna chased Darcy, been unable to catch her before she took off in her vehicle, then returned to the cabin?

He hurried to catch up to Chief Hernandez Sam, and Max, noticed them frowning at the extra footprints, too. The chief even had her weapon out again.

The walk back to the cabin didn't take long—it was a straight line compared to the curved, roundabout route through the woods. But the frigid wind picked up and made him shiver harder, made it seem much farther than it really was. When they finally arrived, Tate was shivering by the road. Chance stood next to him, pressed up against his side as if trying to warm him.

"Did Alanna come back this way?" Peter asked. "And why are you out here? Why didn't you warm up in my truck?" Peter glanced around, realized it wasn't there and asked, "Did some of the officers take it back? Is everyone okay?" Was Alanna okay? Where was she?

"Everyone's fine," Tate said, his teeth actually chattering. "But it's not us who took the truck."

"What do you mean?"

"Apparently, while you were still digging me out and the chief was busy watching the front of the cabin, Alanna ran back from the road and took it."

Peter frowned, realizing that Darcy had been gone long before they'd tried to track her through the woods. That meant Alanna had been climbing into his truck instead of running into the snow to help him pull out Tate.

Tate shivered harder, wrapping his arms around himself. "Nate and Charlie said she was alone. I guess they thought it was okay, since she'd been on your side the last time they saw her."

"She's still on my side," Peter said, although suddenly, he wasn't sure.

Chief Hernandez shook her head and holstered her weapon, heading past them toward her vehicle. Sam and Max followed.

Peter just continued to stare at his partner, trying to understand. Why would Alanna come back here but not wait for him? Why would she take his truck but not explain herself to any of the officers?

At least she was okay. She wasn't a hostage. She wasn't dead.

But if she'd taken his truck, she was trying to chase Darcy down alone.

"We need to catch up to her," he told Tate. "She could be in trouble."

"Right now, we all need to warm up and change or we won't be good for anything." Tate stroked Chance's head with hands that shook. "Since Alanna took off, maybe we can make Chance here our K-9 representative."

Tate had been trying to convince the chief they needed a K-9 unit for as long as Peter had known him. The chief had always countered that the department barely had enough money to pay for officers and their training, let alone add dogs to the mix. Maybe today would change her mind.

Chance looked up at Tate, then over at Peter, as if asking where Alanna was.

"We'll find her, boy," Peter told him.

"Robak! Emory! Get over here," the chief called from inside her SUV. The rest of the officers were already crammed inside. "I'm driving you to the spot the other vehicles were hidden before this unsuccessful raid."

Peter felt himself jerk at the term *raid*. The plan had been for the other officers to be backup, in case things went south. Not for them to jump into action from the outset. Hadn't it?

He glanced sideways at Tate, wondering if anyone else had noticed the slipup. Or if his partner would look guilty for hiding the true nature of their "help." But Tate was just striding toward the SUV, looking miserable.

Still, his fellow officers had hidden in the woods. They'd obviously waited while Peter and Alanna tried to talk Darcy down. Maybe a raid had been a last resort if the negotiation soured. Or maybe they would have run straight in if it had been clear they could get to the kids safely.

"No one who was in the avalanche is driving." The

chief looked Peter over as he, Tate and Chance joined her, then added, "Not you, either, Robak."

He took her point. Everyone who'd been buried in the snow—and him, since he'd been hip-deep in it, digging men out—were soaked and freezing. Although all he felt was miserably cold, the rest of the team might have had their core temperatures drop enough to make driving dangerous.

Last night, even after waiting until they'd warmed up some, Alanna had still been violently shaking as she'd navigated those mountain roads. Thinking about her made him anxious to get moving and he yanked open the back door.

Tate's eyebrows raised as they saw how crowded it already was. "I don't think we're getting two more men and a St. Bernard in there. Why don't you come back for us?"

The chief scowled at him, then the back seat, then finally nodded. "We'll be fast. The vehicles are less than a mile away. I want everyone who was in the avalanche checked out at the hospital."

When most of the officers grumbled, she snapped, "No arguments." Then the back door was slammed shut and the SUV was off, kicking up snow.

"Were you planning to surround me, Darcy and Alanna no matter what?" Peter demanded as soon as they were alone.

Tate turned to him, his lips still tinged blue, his face still too pale. "Are you kidding? Look what just happened here, man. *Your backup* hid and waited for your signal. Did you even see us out there?"

When Peter shook his head, Tate continued. "Yet somehow, Darcy knew. How do you think that happened?"

Anger heated him. He knew the rest of the team had already been thinking it. But he and Tate weren't just partners; they were friends. Tate should have trusted his judgment. "You're insinuating that Alanna tipped her off?"

Chance glanced from him to Tate, as if waiting for the reply, too.

Tate sighed, shaking his head. "She *stole* your truck. Why do you think she did that? Maybe she was trying to slow you down so you couldn't catch up to Darcy and she's mad you brought backup. Or she's been talking to Darcy from the start and she couldn't shake you, so she just brought you along and told Darcy what was going down."

Peter took an aggressive step forward and Chance, sitting between them, got to his feet, looking wary. The dog nudged his arm, as if telling him to calm down.

Peter absently pet Chance, trying to reassure him as he snapped at Tate, "Alanna didn't even know you'd be here. What happened to you thinking Alanna was genuine, that she was trying to help us?"

"Maybe she was," Tate replied, not looking at all threatened by Peter invading his personal space. "But maybe she had second thoughts. Let's be honest here. You cut her out by calling us in secretly. But that doesn't mean she didn't figure out what you were doing. Was she ever alone? Did she ever have a chance to warn

Darcy before you two came out here? She probably didn't expect Darcy to shoot at us, but—"

"Alanna would *never* tip off Darcy. She'd never put those kids in danger."

"Wouldn't they have been in less danger if she'd told the police what she knew as soon as she found those locations? You have to admit it—she still loves Darcy. She's still trying to protect her. What happened to *you* thinking she had some warped loyalty to her kidnappers?"

"I got to know her," Peter said softly, backing up a step as his shoulders slumped. If even Tate didn't believe in Alanna now, what would happen if they caught up to Darcy and Alanna was with her?

Tate nodded, the anger on his face softening as he stared at Peter. "You care about her." It was a statement rather than a question. "But look around here. She took your truck. She hasn't tried to contact you. She even left her dog." He gestured to Chance, who whined and lay on the snowy ground.

"She's not coming back."

CHANCE LOOKED UP from the spot he'd claimed on the floor of the Desparre police station and gave a low whine.

They hadn't heard from Alanna in five hours and Peter definitely wasn't the only one feeling anxious over it. He leaned down and petted the St. Bernard to comfort him.

"He really shouldn't be in here," Chief Hernandez said, but she sighed and petted him, too.

The chief couldn't be too stern with the dog who'd just saved half her force from an avalanche. The same couldn't be said of the way she was treating him. *Furious* was an understatement. He wasn't sure if it was because he'd tried to outpace them in the woods to reach Alanna first or because of everything that had gone wrong the moment they'd driven up to that tiny cabin.

She straightened and peered over his shoulder at his computer. "Any luck?"

Since they'd returned to the station, he'd been trying to figure out the other locations Darcy might have gone. Last night, he'd given Alanna a tiny notebook to jot down whatever she could remember of the list she'd found at the cabin. She'd spent over an hour writing things down and crossing them out until she'd finally gone to bed. While she'd slept, he'd slipped into the guest room and snagged the notebook off the side table.

He'd tried not to look at her at all, feeling like he was invading her privacy, but he hadn't been able to stop himself. The sheets had been twisted beneath her, her long hair tangled around her face, her eyes moving rapidly underneath her eyelids as she dreamed. Was she reliving the avalanche, he'd wondered? Dreaming of her past? Or worrying about Darcy and those kids?

In that moment, he'd had the absurd desire to curl up with her and chase away her nightmares. Then Chance had walked over and Peter had realized the big dog had been watching him from the floor beside Alanna's bed. He'd given the dog a quick pet, told him everything was fine and gone into the other room to copy the contents of the notebook.

The mix of odd symbols, numbers and blank lines—
where presumably Alanna had been trying to remember what she'd seen—hadn't meant much to him last
night. They didn't mean much more now. She'd translated some of the code, but not enough.

He shook his head. "Sorry."

"Luna police haven't had a single sighting."

Apparently they'd been notified about what was happening less than five minutes after Peter had contacted
Tate. It made sense; the cabin was in Luna PD's jurisdiction. But it still bothered him that so quickly after
he'd called for backup, it seemed like everyone knew
what was going on. It made him wonder if there was
some other reason Darcy had been tipped off, like she'd
spotted Luna patrols driving by too often before the
Desparre team had arrived.

Still, once the Desparre officers had headed to the
hospital after the avalanche, Luna's had swept in. Their
PD had set up roadblocks to search for Darcy. Although
no one had mentioned it to him, Peter suspected they'd
been told to stop Alanna, too. He hadn't protested. He
would have been happy if they'd held her, prevented her
from catching up to Darcy on her own.

By now, Alanna was either still following Darcy in
his truck or she'd lost her and was back to following
the list of coordinates. Peter refused to consider the
other possibility: that she'd caught up to Darcy and the
woman had hurt her.

Peter stared down at the notes he'd taken from
Alanna's room. The truth was, he had a couple of
guesses, coordinates he'd worked out based on what

she'd written. But that was all they were—guesses that could be dead-on or hundreds of miles off course.

His chief narrowed her eyes at him, like she knew what he was thinking and wanted the specifics anyway. Before he could admit he had some possibilities, she told him, "According to the hospital, all of the officers are okay. Most of them are heading back to the station now."

"*Most* of them?"

"They're hanging onto Tate a bit longer. His core body temperature was a little low when he came in and they don't want to take any chances."

Peter swore and Chance came over to drop his head onto Peter's lap. Absently stroking the dog's fur, Peter realized how much Chance relaxed him, eased his worry over his partner and Alanna.

Chief Hernandez looked from him to the St. Bernard and back again. "Luna PD isn't too happy with how everything shook out today. I think they're wishing they'd said no to our request to handle it. They think it's time to put out a message to the public, enlist their help."

"Okay," Peter said slowly. "But I thought we were holding off on that in case it escalated things."

"It's been five hours," the chief reminded him. "Darcy got through our checkpoints, probably before we even had them up. If Alanna hasn't been in contact by now, she's not going to be."

"Maybe she can't. Her phone could have—"

"Peter." She said his name with a sigh and a tone of finality. "When Darcy fired into that mountain, Alanna made a choice. She *left* all those officers, including you."

"She went after the kids! She—"

"If she was on our side, we would have heard from her by now." Chief Hernandez put up a hand, as if to forestall the argument she knew was coming. "Maybe she's in trouble. Maybe she's already dead."

Chance whined and got to his feet. Peter's insides twisted until he felt himself hunch over from the pain of it.

"I'm sorry," the chief said. "You've gotten too close to this. At this point, we have to consider Alanna an accessory to kidnapping."

Peter jerked to a standing position, knocking his chair backward and making Chance step sideways out of the way. "She'd never actually *help* Darcy get away with those kids!" No matter how much she loved that woman, that would never happen.

"Peter, look around. Your partner is in the hospital and Alanna left her dog behind. She's gone."

"She's coming back. She'd never leave Chance. She hung on to him in an avalanche!"

"I'm sorry," Chief Hernandez repeated. "But it's time. We're going public with this and we're naming Alanna, too."

She gave him one last look, full of apology and residual anger and just a hint of distrust. Then she disappeared into her office and Peter sank back into his chair.

Chance promptly nuzzled up against him with so much force it pushed the chair backward, his whine a half growl, half cry.

"I know, boy," Peter whispered. "This is bad."

He stared at the chief's closed office door, then over at the few other officers in the station, who were studiously ignoring him. He blew out a long breath and stood. "Come on, boy."

Grabbing his coat, Peter strode for the door, trying not to run. Chance stayed right on his heels. With every step, he could feel the new career he'd fought so hard for slipping away.

But did he really have a choice? Alanna wasn't guilty. And he couldn't let her get hurt because she was trying to make amends for something that wasn't her fault.

It was time to break ranks. It was time to search for Alanna on his own.

Chapter Eleven

Maybe Darcy hadn't been as guilty as Alanna had feared.

Not that she was totally innocent. She'd escaped from law enforcement, fled across the country to hide. But for the first time, Alanna wondered if Darcy had been incorrectly blamed.

Had she really kidnapped those kids?

Alanna stared at the cell phone she'd been holding for the past ten minutes, at Peter's direct contact that he'd entered yesterday. She was sitting in his truck, the truck she'd *stolen*, with the engine running in a tiny back alley on the outskirts of Desparre as the sun began to set.

Five years ago, in the process of trying to find her, Kensie had run into trouble with a criminal. Alanna had first seen her in this alley, from the rearview window of a car as it drove away. For the second time in her life, she'd watched her big sister screaming for her, but in the alley, it had been Kensie who was in trouble. Until her sister had appeared at the cabin, Alanna had thought Kensie had been killed here. Things had turned out okay then, but would they now?

Her phone had rung repeatedly for the past five hours, Peter's name lighting up on her screen. When the first call came in, she'd been on Darcy's tail, too scared to take her eyes off the vehicle for a second. She'd caught up to it a few miles away from the cabin. She hadn't actually been able to see Darcy inside it, but the way the vehicle was speeding, taking corners much too fast, who else could it be?

An hour later, after she'd lost the vehicle—at that point not even sure it was Darcy she'd been chasing— she'd thought about calling Peter. But she hadn't been ready to admit defeat yet. And she'd been terrified to learn what happened to the officers who'd been buried under that avalanche.

When the snow had first started rushing down that mountainside, she'd considered staying for about ten seconds. Peter had already been running toward it, Chance outpacing him. She'd known Chance would be better help digging people out than she would. Darcy had been right in front of her, running back into the cabin, ready to grab those kids and make them disappear again. At least, that was what she'd thought.

Alanna had felt like she was those kids' only shot. She couldn't let Darcy take them again.

Now here she was. Alone. No Darcy. No kids. Afraid to learn what had happened at that cabin.

Setting the phone next to her, Alanna flipped on the radio to a local station. Would this debacle have made the news?

"…officers are doing fine," the host was saying and Alanna relaxed against her seat, grabbing her phone to call Peter, to check on Chance and apologize for all of it. Tell Peter what she'd discovered.

She'd been so sure she could talk some sense into Darcy. Of course, maybe she would have been able to if there hadn't been officers hiding in the woods, signaling to Darcy that Alanna had already betrayed her.

She couldn't totally trust Peter. Not even now, after they'd seemed to connect on such a personal level back at his house. The realization hurt. A lot. But it wasn't the most important thing right now.

Alaska wasn't her home anymore. Soon enough, she'd be back in Chicago, Peter a distant memory. Right now, though, she needed his help. Maybe if she was lucky, if she was right, he could help her prove that Darcy wasn't a kidnapper at all. At least not anymore.

"Be on the lookout for escaped convict Darcy Altier," the radio host continued. "If you see her, contact police immediately. She is armed and dangerous. Police are also looking for her accomplice, Alanna Morgan. In case you don't remember the name, Alanna was one of five children kidnapped by Darcy Altier and her husband nearly twenty years ago. She—"

Alanna flipped the radio off, dropping her phone. The police had named her as an *accomplice*? After she'd told them where to find Darcy? After she'd run into that cabin, trying to rescue those kids, all without any police help?

And after what she'd found…

Darcy had been running out the back door. Alone.

At first, Alanna had thought she'd lucked out. That

Darcy had decided to run and leave the kids behind, avoid putting them in the middle of a standoff.

But a quick search of the one-room cabin had shown Alanna that wasn't the case. Darcy didn't *have* the kids. Maybe she'd never had the kids.

Unfortunately, kidnappings happened all the time. An escaped convict—especially one who'd been in jail for a series of kidnappings—in close enough proximity to a new case would be an obvious suspect. Then, when another kid went missing in a part of Canada that was along a potential route Darcy could take to return to Desparre? Maybe that had been enough to cinch the investigation and Darcy had been innocent all along. This time, anyway.

Alanna would never know unless she found her. It was more obvious than ever that she couldn't trust the police, couldn't trust Peter.

She needed to do this alone.

"IT'S BETTER TO ask forgiveness than permission, right, boy?" Peter asked Chance as he sped them along the icy back streets of Desparre.

Chance's head swiveled in the passenger seat and the look in his eyes suggested he had doubts.

Since Alanna had his truck, Peter had taken his police vehicle. He wasn't sure how long he had before the chief noticed his absence and grew suspicious. Before she called him up and demanded he return to the station. Before he faced serious trouble for ignoring her orders.

Of course, she could track the police vehicle, too, have his fellow officers chase him down. But Peter hadn't had time to find something else. At this point, he was looking at insubordination at best, aiding and abetting a fugitive at worst. What was one borrowed police vehicle in comparison?

Even if he could get away without any charges being brought against him, he was probably finished in Desparre. He'd gotten the job because the department was desperate. Dozens of other applications around the state—even the country—had shown him how fast most police stations would eliminate him without an interview because of his hearing loss.

Unless there was drastic change, his career as a police officer was over. The idea made him nauseous.

Police academy had been brutal. He'd thought he was in good shape before he started, but he'd discovered that traipsing alongside soldiers in war zones hadn't prepared him for the full physicality of chasing suspects for long stretches. It hadn't prepared him for actually carrying his own weapon and learning not to flinch at the sound of it firing, which was just a little too similar to the *boom* of the explosion that had changed his life. It hadn't prepared him for all the small adaptations he had to make just to be sure his bad ear didn't put him or his fellow officers at increased risk.

He'd stuck it out, through the bruises and the flashbacks. He'd even worked through the bullying from an instructor who didn't approve of Desparre PD bending their applicant rules to get another recruit willing to live in their remote town. The guy thought Desparre PD was unnecessarily endangering him—and that Peter could endanger his future colleagues by not being up to the job.

He'd worked hard to be a good officer, to make sure his disability didn't impact his effectiveness. The day he'd graduated from the academy and gotten the official go-ahead to become a Desparre PD rookie, he'd felt a sense of accomplishment and joy headier than his first assignment as a war reporter.

Today he was throwing it all away.

Still, he didn't turn around. No way could he just follow orders when those orders were putting Alanna at risk. No, the only shot he had at saving the career he'd grown to love so much was to bring in Darcy and save those kids.

At least he had an idea where to start. Sure, it was an idea based half on coordinates Alanna had decoded from her memory of the symbols she'd seen, half on guesswork. He had filled in the blanks, considering what else made sense based on the numbers she had and satellite images of the area. But guesswork was better than nothing. It was better than sitting in that station, waiting to hear that police officers in some other town had surrounded Darcy and Alanna. That they'd considered both women dangerous and were willing to sacrifice them in order to save two kidnapped children. That they'd shot first, asked questions later.

The very idea of anyone training a weapon on Alanna made him punch down harder on the gas. The first location he'd worked out wasn't nearby. It was in the total opposite direction of the cabin in Luna, in a town even tinier than Desparre. A place that didn't even

have their own police force. It seemed like the best option for his quarry.

After all, there was no way to know how long he
could run these leads alone before his fellow officers
surrounded his car and demanded he stand down. Demanded he hand over his weapon and his badge.

As if sensing his thoughts, Chance let out a sudden
woof that startled Peter into jerking the wheel. Chance
was jolted in the seat and Peter righted the car on the
slippery ice. "I know, boy. You're my backup today."

Alanna had told him how the St. Bernard had been
rescued from a cruel owner as a puppy, how she'd gotten
him certified as a therapy dog so she could bring him
with her to work. It was as much to help her own anxiety as it was to help the trauma survivors she worked
with, she'd said. Chance had known exactly when to
comfort him at the police station, even when to support
Tate out in the cold by the cabin; it was clear he was a
damn good therapy dog. And given the way he'd raced
into action during the avalanche, he probably would
have made a good police dog, too.

"We'll find her," Peter told him, hoping it was true.

Chance whined softly, turning his attention out the
front windshield. The dog seemed as desperate to find
Alanna as Peter.

And he *was* desperate. There was no other word for it.

Four days ago, he would have scoffed at the idea that
he could come to trust Alanna Morgan, let alone that
he would care for her so much. But at his house, they'd
connected. It had lifted a weight off him to be able to
open up about his past. And he'd come to admire her

fortitude after everything she'd experienced. If she lived in Alaska, if she wasn't part of an ongoing case, he'd already be pursuing her romantically. The idea felt ridiculous and yet it made him yearn for something he hadn't realized was missing from his life.

Maybe it wasn't Alanna. Maybe it was just time for him to think about finding someone to settle down with, like all his older siblings. Have some kids, make a real home. Take down those pictures from war zones on his walls and move forward. Except how could he do that if he didn't even have a job?

He shook off the worries he couldn't be distracted by right now and slowed as he approached the coordinates he'd mapped out. He'd looked up the location online, zoomed in and seen what might have been a cabin. Perhaps it was a hiding spot for a desperate couple who'd known one day their crimes could catch up to them. Who'd suspected they would eventually be on the run again.

Adrenaline shot through him as he drove slowly past. It was hard to tell now that the sun was down, but up close, he realized there *was* a cabin. Tiny and tucked away from the street behind more woods, it looked a lot like the place in Luna from this afternoon. It was a well-built log cabin, similar in style to the house where the Altiers had lived in Desparre, the one they'd built by hand. Could Julian have built this place himself, too? Peter could see light through the windows.

This time he didn't slow down, didn't pull into the driveway. He drove right past and parked down the road where his vehicle wouldn't be visible from the cabin.

For one crazy second, he considered calling for backup. But even though he and Tate had developed a strong friendship outside of work, he couldn't ask his friend to risk his career. Besides, Peter didn't even know if Tate was out of the hospital yet. And there was no one else he'd trust to protect Alanna no matter what they saw, no matter what happened.

"It's you and me, boy," he told Chance, his breath puffing in front of him as he stepped out of the vehicle. His boots broke through a top layer of ice with a noisy crunch, then sank down into more than a foot of snow beneath. He hoped he wasn't making a mistake letting the dog come, but he couldn't just leave him in the SUV, hidden out here in the woods. What would happen if Peter was killed and no one knew he was here?

Chance leaped out of the vehicle, sticking close and moving silently. His big body was hunched over, the fur on his back raised, like he was stalking something. Like he knew exactly what they were doing and he, too, was willing to risk everything for Alanna.

"Be careful," Peter whispered, simultaneously hoping that the dog understood and that Darcy wouldn't hurt Alanna's pet.

Chance glanced at him once, then looked back toward the cabin. The dog was focused and slinking forward as if he knew Alanna was in there.

Hoping he was right, Peter unholstered his pistol and crept slowly along beside Chance, toward the home. He moved from the cover of one tree to the next, cursing the wind that whistled past his ears as it limited his hearing even further. The snow was deeper here than it had been in Luna and the damp cold seeping through his jeans above the tops of his boots made him shiver. But at least the icy top layer was more melted here, his boots making a quieter *crunch* each time they broke through.

A shadow moved behind the curtains in one of the windows and Peter's pulse jumped. It didn't mean he'd found them, but *someone* was home.

He scanned the area and spotted something on the far side of the cabin, a brief reflection of light in the moonlight. Squinting at it, he realized with a start that it was his truck. Alanna was here.

Creeping closer, he reached the edge of the woods, then made a run for the side of the cabin, staying in a crouch. Chance raced along beside him, reaching the cabin first. But he waited for Peter, giving him a look that seemed to ask, *What's the plan?*

Flattening himself against the side of the cabin, Peter peered at the window, hoping for a gap in the curtains. There was nothing to see, so he tapped his thigh for Chance to follow and slunk to the back of the dwelling. He wasn't worried about Chance barking. The dog was well-trained and seemed to sense the need to stay silent.

The windows here were the same, but just like the last cabin, there was a back door. For a building this small, it didn't really need more than one entrance. Unless someone needed an easy escape route.

Peter tested the handle, expecting it to be locked. But it moved under his hand and he froze, hoping no one inside had seen it. For a moment, indecision gripped him, made all his muscles tense. Then he eased the door slowly open, angling his weapon so he could lead with it.

Though it probably wouldn't help; doorways were one of the most dangerous places for police officers. You didn't know what was on the other side, and the only way to find out if someone was standing there waiting with their own weapon drawn was to open the door and go inside.

He'd trained for this, Peter reminded himself. Sure, if he was here officially, he'd have a partner. But someone would still have to go through first. In police academy, you learned a simple series of steps to get you inside and out of a doorway as fast as possible. You learned the exact sequence your gun hand and your attention should move to eliminate any threats before they could eliminate you. Still, none of that changed the fact that dying as you came through a doorway was far too common for police officers.

He weighed calling out "police," but thought it too risky. If Darcy was holding Alanna and the children, he could put them in jeopardy by alerting her to his presence.

He glanced sideways at Chance, who was waiting in a crouched stance as if he planned to bound in after Peter, and held up a hand, telling the dog to wait. Then he steadied his gun hand, ignored the senses-dimming staccato of his heartbeat and pushed the door wide.

The tiny kitchen he stepped into was empty, but beyond an open doorway, he could hear voices. One of them belonged to Alanna.

"I *believed* in you," she was saying, the hurt palpable in her words. "After all this time, I really thought that if I could just talk to you, make you understand, that you'd—"

"What?" Darcy interrupted, the volume of her own anger and hurt dwarfing Alanna's. "Turn myself in? Go back to jail? *Die there*, like your father did?"

"That's the thing," Alanna said, her tone sad but strong. "As much as you wanted to be, as much as I loved you both, you weren't my parents. And—"

Darcy made a sound that was half furious screech, half wounded cry.

This wasn't going anywhere good. Peter darted around the doorway, handgun raised, hoping to find Darcy distracted and across the room from Alanna.

Before he'd fully entered the room, though, Darcy spun toward him, her own pistol raised.

"You shouldn't have come here," Darcy spat.

Peter aimed his gun at her head—instead of her center mass, like he'd been taught. He did a quick visual sweep—Alanna across the room, unarmed, her hands up in the air as if she'd been trying to calm Darcy down. But Alanna wasn't his problem right now.

It was the little boy on the floor, clutching Darcy's leg and staring at him wide-eyed. It was the little girl held in the crook of Darcy's arm, silent tears running down her face as Darcy used her as a human shield.

Chapter Twelve

"Please, just put the gun down," Alanna begged.

"Him again!" Darcy snapped. "What happened to all your promises that it was just the two of us talking? It's always lies with you, isn't it?"

Alanna swallowed the desire to snap back, to argue about who was lying to who. She'd never seen Darcy like this. All her life, Darcy had been full of smiles and ideas and plans she couldn't always see through. She was flighty and occasionally depressed, but she was always patient with the kids she'd called hers.

When Alanna had entered the second cabin in Luna, she'd been amazed. She'd thought it was a sign that things were about to go right. That even though Darcy had escaped from prison, she hadn't returned to kidnapping. That there was a chance to end it all peacefully.

She'd been so wrong.

Maybe Julian's death had unhinged Darcy. Or maybe Alanna had only seen what she'd wanted to see all those years she'd lived with her. Maybe Peter had been right and she'd been brainwashed by a pair of kidnappers.

"She didn't know I was coming," Peter said, his voice

calm and soft as Chance walked slowly into the cabin behind him and came to a stop at his side.

The dog's gaze moved from Alanna to the kids, then back to Peter, as if awaiting instructions.

Tension knotted tighter in Alanna's chest. How had Peter found them? Why would he bring Chance into this?

She tried to tell him with her eyes to stay out of it, to let her try to reach Darcy. Her gaze darted to the kids, the small girl in Darcy's arms with dark, curly hair that reminded Alanna so much of herself as a child. The little boy clutching Darcy's leg with the deep brown eyes and the short dark hair. Both of them could have easily passed as Altiers.

"Do you know how much I miss you?" Darcy asked, her voice breaking as Alanna's gaze returned to hers. "Do you know how much I miss all of you? Do you know what it was like to have my kids ripped away from me?"

"I'm—" Alanna started.

"Do you know how badly it hurt to know it was *you* who set it all in motion? What it feels like to have you tell me I'm not your mom?" She let out a humorless laugh. "I know I'm not your mom. Not legally. I…" She shook her head, staring through Alanna now, her brow furrowed like she was peering into the past.

"I could never have kids," Darcy admitted softly. She tipped her head against the child in her arms and the little girl hugged her neck.

She obviously felt safe with Darcy, despite everything. It was what Alanna had felt right from the start, too. Irrational, maybe, but she'd instinctively known she was loved.

A surge of hope hit, a gut feeling that she could still reach Darcy, still talk her into ending this peacefully. Because no matter what else might have changed, the Darcy she'd known for fourteen years was still in there. A Darcy who would never hurt kids she'd decided were hers. But Peter… If Darcy thought he was a threat, she'd fire at him the way she'd shot at Kensie all those years ago.

She hadn't done it when she could have at the cabin in Luna, a tiny voice whispered in the back of her mind. It was a voice Alanna couldn't trust, a voice that had been born from her past life. Still, it was a past life where Darcy had raised her to be strong, had hugged her every night before bed, had greeted her every morning with love.

"I'm sorry," Alanna said.

"My family never understood me," Darcy continued, not seeming to notice Peter as he shifted just slightly to angle his good ear toward her. His weapon, too.

Chance moved too, surprisingly stealthy for such a big dog, sticking to Peter's side as if they were a team with a shared plan.

Praying that Peter would just wait, that Chance wouldn't think she was in trouble and try coming to her rescue, Alanna nodded encouragingly at Darcy. She'd never met anyone from Darcy or Julian's families. When she was younger, it hadn't occurred to her to wonder why. When she was older, she'd assumed it was because of the kidnappings, because of the Altiers' constant reminders that it was the seven of them against the world. But maybe they'd been estranged long before that.

"They were all overachievers, every one of them. They couldn't stand failure," Darcy said. "Me? I had so much trouble learning. But Julian always accepted me just as I was. When we got married, I wanted our life to be so different from the way I'd grown up. We always talked about having a big family, raising them differently. So when we couldn't have kids, I was devastated. We tried to adopt. A little boy, the age Johnny would have been then. It was such a long process and we finally got to the end of it. He was supposed to come home with us over the weekend. Then that Friday, the adoption fell through. He went back to his biological family. They were drug addicts, in and out of rehab, in and out of prison, but somehow they convinced a judge they should get one more chance to be parents."

The sadness and loss on her face shifted to anger. "Four weeks later, he was dead. Killed in a house fire his parents had set while they were high. And we just couldn't do it. We couldn't go through it again. We gave up on adoption."

"So you took Johnny?" Alanna recalled what she'd read about his abduction in the papers years later. "From the park when his mom was distracted, right?"

"She wasn't even watching him," Darcy said, a new light in her eyes, the spark of a past joy. "Julian said it had been easy to pick him off the swings and bring him home to me. Johnny didn't even cry. It was like he wanted to come to us, like it was meant to be. But afterward…" She frowned, shook her head, glanced at Peter.

Her eyes narrowed and Alanna was sure she'd noticed that Peter was just slightly closer, that Chance was edging closer, too. "Afterward?" Alanna pressed.

"It was such a mix of emotions," Darcy said, happiness back in her eyes. "Probably what it feels like right after you've given birth to a child. Elation like you've never felt, but fear, too. Almost terror, really. And the guilt…" She leaned into the little girl she held and her gun hand, still aimed at Peter, shook a little.

She'd always known it was wrong. Alanna had wondered for years whether Darcy and Julian had felt any regret for taking her and her "siblings." If Darcy had felt guilty then, surely the guilt was intensified now, knowing that the kids who'd gone home to their families had missed them for years.

If she had any regret, felt any guilt, then Alanna could still reach her. She took a step forward, her hand out toward Darcy.

"A few years later, when we saw you…"

Alanna froze and her heart seemed to contract. It was a moment she remembered so distinctly and yet she'd never known how they'd picked her, or why.

"The first time I saw you, I just *knew.* You looked so much like I did as a child, but it was more than that. I just felt it, deep inside, that you were meant to be my daughter." Her eyes glassed over with unshed tears. "I still feel that, Alanna."

Alanna took another step closer until she could almost touch Darcy, almost reach out and push the gun down. "In some ways, I'll always be your daughter." The words were shaky with emotion, because they were true.

The smile Alanna had seen every day of her childhood blossomed on Darcy's face and the woman's rigid arm loosened, the gun angling downward, away from Peter.

Alanna slid forward just a tiny bit more. "But the Morgans weren't drug addicts. They loved me. They spent so many years searching for me. They were even called into more than one morgue for identifications that turned out not to be me."

The smile slid from Darcy's face. Alanna could see the guilt there as her "mom" glanced down at the little boy still hugging tightly to her leg.

"My older sister almost died trying to find me. My older brother turned to drugs and alcohol and anything else he could find because losing me tore my family apart. They didn't deserve that," Alanna said, sliding forward again. Just one more step…

"I know," Darcy whispered.

Hope erupted inside Alanna, a happiness that she hadn't been wrong about Darcy; that even though the woman had kidnapped her, there was still good in her, still reasons why Alanna had grown to love her.

Darcy was still a criminal. Once she returned to jail, Alanna would have to consider whether to see her again. She'd stolen the childhood Alanna had been meant to have. And yet, that fact didn't erase the fourteen years of love, the happy childhood Darcy and Julian *had* given her. It didn't change the fact that even though Alanna had gone home to the Morgans, even though she didn't regret it, she still loved Darcy, too.

Maybe that was something Alanna needed to stop feeling guilty about.

"You have to let these kids go," Alanna said.

Darcy's face immediately shuttered, the hand holding the gun shaking.

Alanna stepped closer, put her hand on the top of the pistol and said, "You know it's the right thing to do. Please."

The weapon shook violently underneath Alanna's hand, the fight happening within Darcy written all over her face. Then her shoulders slumped and Alanna smiled gently, knowing she'd won.

The sudden grumble of an old car engine from somewhere nearby startled her, made Chance let out a soft *woof*.

In an instant, the indecision on Darcy's face was gone, replaced by an angry determination as she took a fast step backward. The little boy stumbled along with her, the little girl lifting her head as Darcy stiffened her arm and leveled her gun on Peter.

"Don't," Peter warned softly. "I'm a trained police officer. My aim is better than yours."

Betrayal flashed across Darcy's face, but she didn't glance Alanna's way this time. Instead she stared directly at Peter, the guilt in her voice shifting to anger. "You want to find out? You're a bigger target than I am. At this distance, I could be a terrible shot and still kill you. You want to risk being slightly off your mark and hitting my girl?"

Chance let out a low growl, took a slow step forward with his front paw.

Alanna held up a hand and he froze. She didn't dare look at Peter.

She had no idea what Peter's training was like, how accurate a shot he was. She doubted he'd fire unless he had to with the little girl in Darcy's arms.

But five years ago, Darcy had fired at Kensie. And she hadn't aimed to wound.

Darcy's head tipped back slightly, her lips tightening as if she'd made a decision, and panic took hold of Alanna.

She leaped in between them, spreading her arms wide.

"Alanna!" Peter yelled, a mix of anger and fear in his voice as he shifted sideways and she moved with him. "Get out of the way!"

Alanna didn't take her gaze off of Darcy.

A ghost of a smile lifted one corner of Darcy's mouth, a sad understanding look in her eyes, before she spun and escaped out the front door with the little girl.

"Chance, stay!" Alanna yelled as she practically body-slammed Peter.

Peter slid his finger off the trigger, bracing himself to absorb her weight so he wouldn't get knocked to the ground. "What are you doing? She's getting away!"

"She could kill you!" The panic in Alanna's voice was unmistakable, the desperation clear in the surprising strength of her grip as she wrapped her arms around his waist and hung on.

He swore, angling his gun away from her as he tried to push her away with his free hand. Alanna was a lot stronger than she looked, with lean muscle in her arms and legs and a good knowledge of leverage that she used to her advantage.

He glanced at the closed door. "If she gets away now, how will we find her? She's got a child!"

"Darcy won't hurt her, but she'll hurt you," Alanna said, her fingers digging into him, her desperation dangerous.

He didn't want to hurt Alanna. But the cough and sputter of a car's engine followed by the squeal of tires made him swear. "I'm sorry," he said, and twisted her arm as if he was going to push her to the ground and arrest her. The move broke her grip on him, prevented her from twisting back. Then he pushed her away and darted for the door, hoping he wasn't too late to stop Darcy.

Alanna ran after him and he spun back, holding his pistol away from his body, afraid it would accidentally fire as she grappled him. But she wasn't coming for him this time.

She reached for the little boy Darcy had left behind, who'd been crying since the melee had started and now ran toward the door, too, to follow the woman who'd kidnapped him.

Chance got there first, blocking the boy's way and plopping onto the floor. He knocked the boy down with him, but instead of crying harder, the little boy wrapped his arms around the big dog and buried his head in Chance's fur.

Alanna sighed, then looked up at Peter, fear and regret in her eyes.

She had to know he wouldn't hurt Darcy unless there was no other choice, didn't she? He wanted to reassure her that everything would be okay, but it wasn't a promise he could make, so he just broke eye contact and took off out the door.

The yard seemed empty, moonlight filtering through the towering trees and iced-over snow. But there were a lot of places to hide and no guarantee the engine he'd heard was actually Darcy's. Would she have been able to get into a vehicle that fast? He hadn't seen any other vehicles except his own truck when he'd arrived. The trees here were thick; there probably wasn't enough space to hide a vehicle except close to the road.

His heart thudded too fast as he tried to focus on any sound that didn't belong, any movement in his peripheral vision. But the woods were too dark, the diminished hearing in his left ear made worse by the stress of knowing Darcy could be hunkered down behind a nearby tree, taking careful aim at him.

A crunch that could have been someone stepping through the icy snow made him swivel his head right, toward the direction of his parked police vehicle. He squinted through the darkness, trying to spot any movement, then a quiet *snap* from the left made his head swivel. Animals? Darcy sneaking up on him, ready to eliminate the only other person with a weapon?

If he was shot in these woods, what would Alanna do? Rush out and try to help him while Darcy took aim at her, took her revenge for Alanna's betrayal, and then disappeared with both kids?

Furious to be in this position, Peter backed slowly toward the cabin, slipping inside. He shut the door, holstered his weapon and pulled out his phone.

"What happened?" Alanna demanded from where she was crouched on the floor, her arms around both Chance and the little boy.

"I can't see anything. Do you know where she parked?"

Alanna shook her head. "I didn't see a vehicle."

He pulled Chief Hernandez up on his phone, but Alanna was by his side, gripping his arm, before he could hit Call.

"What are you doing?" She sounded panicked, like she was still thinking with emotion instead of logic.

For a few brief moments, he'd thought her raw emotion and honesty were what would change Darcy's mind and end this whole thing peacefully. But that time had passed. Now they needed logic. And manpower.

He pulled his hand free and did the thing he should have done from the start. "We need backup."

When Chief Hernandez answered the phone, he gave her a quick rundown of their location and status, then turned back to Alanna.

She was staring wide-eyed at him, the shock on her face mixed with grief.

Knowing she'd just lost a piece of her childhood, he squeezed her hand gently as he told her, "Lock the door behind me. Stay here with the boy and Chance."

Chance stood at his name, took a step toward Peter, then looked at the closed door. As if he was ready to run out with Peter or stand between a threat and Alanna.

"Good boy, Chance," he said, then looked sternly at Alanna. "Don't let anyone in except the Desparre PD."

He didn't mention that they considered her an accomplice and might arrest her when they arrived. He and Alanna would have to deal with that if it happened. Instead, he let go of her hand and turned for the door when her fingers latched onto his arm again. When he turned back, there was regret on her face.

"Back at the other cabin, when I chased after her, I was so sure I could catch her. I thought if it was just the two of us, I could talk her down."

"I know," Peter said, peeling her fingers away. He pulled out his weapon again, glancing at her before he moved to slip out the door. The pink flush of emotion across her pale cheeks and the sadness in her dark eyes were a split-second image he knew would stick with him long after she was gone.

He'd risked his career for her. Risked his life for her. He had no regrets about that, but he'd still been wrong tonight.

If he'd let his team in on what he was doing, he would have had backup right now. There would have been a team waiting outside the cabin, ready to surround Darcy and talk her down, or follow at a distance until they could bring in reinforcements to take her out and protect the little girl.

Instead, Darcy was gone again. He and Alanna had the boy, but what about the little girl?

Peter forced himself not to look back at Alanna, at the sorrow and regret in her eyes. He closed the door behind him, his eyes slowly adjusting to the darkness. He hoped it wasn't already too late, but his gut told him it was.

He'd sacrificed his job thinking he was doing the right thing for everyone, Alanna in particular. But had his mistake just cost a little girl the chance to grow up with her real family?

Chapter Thirteen

The subtle *clack clack clack* of metal against metal echoed through the woods and Peter froze, his arms tense as they supported his pistol. The noise was coming from his right, in the direction of where he'd parked.

In an instant, he realized what it was. The sound of someone trying to open the door to his police SUV. He didn't pause to wonder why Darcy would be trying to get into his vehicle instead of racing for her own. He just started running.

The deeper he went into the woods, the icier the top layer of snow got, crunching as he set each foot down, trying to suck his boots off as he lifted them back up. His breath puffed out in front of him in frigid blasts of air, his lungs feeling every degree that had dropped in the past few hours, every moment he'd spent earlier today digging his friends out of the snow.

As he got closer to the SUV, he slowed, knowing his heavy footsteps in the snow were telegraphing his approach. He couldn't hear Darcy anymore. But was it because she'd gone silent, listening to his approach and trying to line him up in her sights in the darkness? Or just because his hearing wasn't good enough to make out the soft noise of her slinking away over his own footsteps?

He ducked against the shelter of a big tree trunk just before the *boom* of a gun rang out. The muzzle flash told him she was standing behind his vehicle, using it as cover.

His heart thumped at the near miss, then with a realization. Darcy had run the wrong way out of the cabin. Unless he'd totally missed it, there was no other vehicle out this way. She must have left her car in the other direction. To get to it, she'd have to slip past him. Instead of taking the risk, she'd tried to take his vehicle.

He didn't need to rush her now, try to get close through the threat of more bullets. He just needed to pin her there, prevent her from flanking him and returning to her own vehicle. Then he could wait her out, because the rest of his team was on their way. With sirens and lights, they should arrive in less than ten minutes.

Sliding farther behind the tree trunk, Peter squeezed his eyes shut and focused on his hearing. He angled his good ear toward the vehicle, straining to hear any sound that would indicate Darcy was on the move. But he heard nothing.

The muzzle flash had left a temporary mark on his retinas and he waited, listening, until it went away. Then he opened his eyes again and shapes that had been indistinct before became identifiable. A stray branch, broken and dangling from the tree in front of him. Holes in the snow, distinctly paw-shaped, where Chance had stalked alongside him on the way to the cabin. Bigger holes where his boots had broken through in his frantic rush to get to Alanna.

Peter leaned slightly around the edge of the tree, leading with his gun, because if his eyes had started to adjust to the darkness, surely Darcy's had, too.

There was nothing. No top of her head peeking over the vehicle, no outstretched hand clutching a pistol, shifting to take aim. No crying little girl, cold and afraid.

A curse formed on his lips as he turned his head, angling his right side the other way to listen for Darcy. Had she given up on her vehicle to head deeper into the woods? Or maybe she had just kept going past his car and to the road, hoping to hitch a ride from someone who didn't recognize her? Was she able to move through the snow more quietly than he could, his hearing loss too great to detect her?

He didn't hear her. But suddenly, he heard sirens, approaching fast.

Then Darcy was racing away from his vehicle, desperation in the extended length of her strides, in the way the child was clutched in her arms.

She held the girl tight with both hands, Peter realized. It meant she didn't have a hand free to aim and fire.

He moved away from the protection of the tree to pursue her. He was taller than her, with longer strides, and he was quickly closing the gap between them. But he couldn't fire without risking the girl, so he holstered his gun.

Darcy glanced back, saw him gaining and put on a new burst of speed.

It wasn't going to be enough, though, and she must

have known it, because she halted suddenly, spinning toward him, her arms shifting to juggle the girl and pull her gun.

He leaped toward her, going for her gun hand. He grabbed it before her finger could slip under the trigger guard and then he was tossing the weapon aside, twisting her arm up and back.

She yelped and the girl, still caught in her other arm, started to cry.

"Hand her over," Peter demanded. Then the sirens were suddenly on top of them, the flashing blue and red lights sweeping over Darcy's face and illuminating the tears there, too.

Chief Hernandez and Tate were running through the woods to meet them, weapons out. Peter felt a wash of relief to see his partner had been discharged from the hospital.

"She's unarmed," he yelled, even though as he said it, he realized he couldn't be sure she didn't have another weapon on her.

Still, he had a hard grip on her arm, had it twisted at such an angle that there was no way for her to move it without causing a break. If she wanted to go for a weapon, she'd have to drop the child. Staring at her now, at her tear-filled eyes, wide and panicked, he knew she wouldn't do it. Because even as she shook her head at the approaching cops, she made soothing *shh* noises under her breath to the child, slightly rocking her. Trying to comfort her.

"Hand her over," Peter repeated, softer this time, as the chief stepped forward, holstering her weapon and holding out her arms. "It will be okay. We'll take care of her. I promise."

Then he heard the crunching of ice behind him, the sound of someone dashing toward them.

Tate shifted his weapon up and over, then returned his aim to Darcy.

Peter glanced over his shoulder and cursed as he saw that it was Alanna. Chance and the boy weren't with her, which meant she'd left them in the cabin. She'd probably heard the sirens, heard him yell to his teammates that Darcy wasn't armed anymore.

Darcy's gaze locked on Alanna and guilt flashed across her face before she dipped her head. Then her shoulders slumped. She stretched her arm with the girl in it toward Chief Hernandez.

The girl clung to Darcy's neck and Chief Hernandez peeled her arms free, tried to soothe her as she cried. The chief stepped backward, unzipping her coat and tucking the child into it as she nodded at Peter.

He grabbed Darcy's other hand and handcuffed her. Then he pushed her against a tree trunk and moved her legs slightly apart with his foot so he could pat her down for additional weapons. "I tossed a pistol that way," he told Tate, gesturing with the jerk of his head the area where he'd knocked it away from Darcy.

Alanna reached them just as he'd confirmed Darcy didn't have any other weapons on her. Alanna was panting from exertion, her gaze darting to Tate, to the pistol he still held as he swept the discarded one out of the snow, and tucked it into his belt.

Peter's partner didn't train his weapon at Alanna,

but as he straightened, he locked eyes with her, ready to take action if she rushed to help Darcy.

"She's no threat," Peter told Tate, hoping it was true. "The boy is in the cabin with Chance."

His partner gave him a tense nod.

Peter had definitely destroyed some trust tonight.

"Why did you run?" Alanna demanded, her focus entirely on Darcy. She stepped forward, getting too close, and Peter forced Darcy backward, toward the police car.

Tate holstered his gun and stepped in front of her, preventing Alanna from getting any closer to Darcy.

Chief Hernandez told Peter, "Put Darcy in my vehicle. You'll bring the kids back to the station. Take Tate with you." Her words were clipped and angry, telling Peter there was a reckoning to come.

Peter nodded and pushed Darcy toward the open door of the police vehicle at the edge of the road.

Alanna's voice trailed after them, gaining volume as she demanded over and over, "*Why? Why? Why?*"

Darcy didn't respond, didn't look back once as Peter put her in the SUV and slammed the door shut.

Then he turned back to the scene behind him. He took in Chief Hernandez smoothing her hand over the girl's hair, whispering quiet words as the girl stared up at her, her tears slowly drying. His gaze skipped to his partner next. Tate stood in front of Alanna, feet braced hip-width apart as if he expected he'd need to forcibly stop her from chasing after them. And then there was Alanna herself, frozen in place, her lips still parted from her last screamed question. The pain on her face was hard to see, but at least their chase was over.

Her methods might not have been ideal, but she'd helped them find Darcy. Ultimately, she was the reason they'd been able to rescue these kids. Without her knowledge of Darcy and how to decode symbols that had looked like nonsense to whoever had gone through the Altiers' home years ago, they never would have found this place.

The kids would be reunited with their families now. Alanna could go home to the family who'd waited so long for her return.

It was where she belonged. Back in Chicago, a town he'd never visited, never wanted to.

He belonged in Desparre, fighting for a job that had given him back his passion. For a team he'd grown to respect, a partnership that had become a friendship. A calling that spoke to him even more than being a reporter. A job that now might be beyond saving.

He hadn't even known Alanna for a full week and they'd spent most of that time at odds. He'd broken her trust by calling in his team at the cabin in Luna. She'd broken his by going after Darcy alone after the woman had caused an avalanche. But he had the sense that Alanna understood his actions, as he did hers. After everything they'd been through, he felt a connection to her that was undeniable.

It had been fast, and yet, he couldn't imagine her leaving. Couldn't imagine losing something he'd only just begun to realize he wanted in his life.

Chapter Fourteen

Alanna drove slowly through downtown Desparre, taking in the snow-lined streets bracketed by a handful of buildings, looking like a postcard for peace and solitude. She was in a new rental car; her forgiving rental company had apparently lost other vehicles to avalanches. And yes, maybe they'd also been angling for juicy details of the new kidnappings from the mouth of someone whose involvement was still a mystery.

The police had given a statement to the press first thing this morning. Alanna had watched it in the darkness of her hotel room after a fitful night of sleeplessness. They'd announced Darcy's arrest and the rescue of the kids. When reporters demanded to know whether Alanna was still at large, the police chief had briskly shared that Alanna was no longer a person of interest, that she hadn't been involved in the kidnappings. Then she'd left the podium, ignoring the reporters' follow-up questions.

Technically, Alanna had been cleared of any wrongdoing. But she knew how this worked. The lack of details meant reporters would be clamoring to talk to her again. They'd start showing up on her doorstep, using creative methods to get into her building, asking invasive questions about her life and her emotions.

After watching the press conference, it had taken another hour for Alanna to get up the courage to leave the hotel and drive into town. But she wanted to see Desparre once more before she went home. She needed to make one stop before she drove to the airport and left Alaska behind, probably for good.

When she'd lived in Desparre, she'd only seen the downtown's main street from the back seat of a car. The Altiers had deemed it too risky to let her or her "siblings" walk around the more populated parts of Desparre, even if "more populated" meant seeing a dozen people.

The small town was beautiful, comforting. It was similar to the smaller section of streets nearer to the cabin where they'd lived, where she *had* been allowed to walk around sometimes. In a lot of ways, Desparre still felt more like her home than Chicago.

But it wasn't. And it was time to leave again.

Five years ago, when she'd stepped onto that plane with Kensie, she'd been terrified of what the future held. Terrified to leave behind everything she'd known for most of her life. But deep down, she'd known she'd done the right thing. This time, she wasn't so sure.

Yes, the kids were safe. But would it have happened sooner if she'd been more open with the police?

From the passenger seat, Chance leaned over and nudged her arm with his wet nose.

When she glanced at him with a fond smile, he gave

her a forceful *woof*, like he knew what was going on in her mind and wanted her to forgive herself.

Darcy was back behind bars. This time, the woman who'd raised her had refused to see *her*. The children she'd kidnapped had been taken to the hospital to be evaluated. Their parents were flying in to be with them, joyous reunions that would get the reporters clamoring again.

They were safe. And they were young enough, the extent of their kidnappings short enough that they wouldn't attract the same kind of sustained media attention she'd faced.

There was nothing left for her here, no more guilt-ridden mission to fulfill. No reason to remain in Desparre any longer. If Darcy wouldn't see her, after everything that had happened, maybe that was for the best. And yet, Alanna felt unsettled, as if she still had unfinished business.

One last apology, she reminded herself, pulling into the parking lot alongside the Desparre police station. One last goodbye.

As if he could read her mind—and didn't like it—Chance gave a soft whine as she opened the door.

"I'm going to miss him, too," she whispered softly, realizing what was causing her anxiety. It wasn't the awkward apology, the thought of all those judging eyes inside the station. She was expecting that; she'd had practice dealing with it. No matter what the official line was, Alanna knew most of the police force was angry with her. For her part in leading them to the site where Darcy had started the avalanche. For going off on her own afterward. For whatever role she'd played in Peter's decision to come to her aid alone.

None of those things were making her heart beat too fast, making dread lodge in her chest. It was the thought of never seeing Peter again.

"We have to do it," she told Chance, forcing herself to get out of the car. She was grateful there weren't any reporters camped out at the police station like they'd been at her hotel; she had needed to slip out the service entrance. But why would there be? They wouldn't expect her to come here.

She owed the whole station an apology. Her intentions might have been good, but when they'd come to help, someone she loved had tried to kill them.

She owed Peter an apology most of all. Even though they had never really been anything except reluctant partners in a search for a kidnapper, it felt like they'd created a friendship. It felt like they'd been on the path to something more.

Chance leaped out of the car to follow her up to the police station the way he'd done the first day she'd returned to Desparre. Had it only been five days ago?

When they'd arrived, his tail had been wagging at the adventure. He'd strode along beside her, then raced off briefly to pounce in the fluffy snow before returning to her side.

Today, his tail faced downward and even his chin was angled to the ground. Either he was catching her mood or he was sad to be leaving this place, too.

"We'll be home soon," she tried to reassure him. "You'll get to play with Rebel."

At the mention of Kensie and Colter's dog, Chance's tail gave a quick wag, but then he was staring ahead again, intent and serious.

Alanna took a deep breath and closed her eyes, trying to relax. But her usual method for coping with anxiety didn't work. Instead, she pictured Peter's face, in turns furious, betrayed and understanding. She could almost feel his long fingers sliding through hers, offering comfort, even as distrust flickered in his eyes.

What might have happened between them if she had a reason to stay longer? If she'd come here for a different purpose entirely? If they were both different people, him without the trauma of standing too close to a hostage who'd blown herself up, her without the baggage of growing up with people who'd kidnapped her?

Maybe nothing. Maybe it was their pasts that had drawn them together, made them both understanding and wary of one another. Maybe the same thing that had created the spark between them would have ultimately destroyed it.

"I guess I'll never know," Alanna whispered, pushing open the door to the station.

The moment she was led into the bullpen where the officers worked, a dozen gazes flicked her way, started to turn back, then fixated on her. Angry, suspicious gazes from officers who'd dug their way out of an avalanche yesterday. Officers who, at minimum, thought she'd wanted a kidnapper to get away and at worst, thought she'd been helping Darcy all along.

"I'm sorry," Alanna said, her voice creaking out, little more than a whisper. She cleared her throat and repeated the words, louder. "I came here because I wanted to help. I came here because I thought I knew Darcy. I thought I understood what she'd do and how I could get through to her. I never wanted anyone to be hurt because of me."

When the officers just continued to stare at her, none of them making a move to accept her apology, heat pricked her cheeks and she ducked her head.

Then Tate was beside her, kindness in his eyes and in the hand he put on her arm. "It's okay, Alanna. It wasn't your fault. We all know that now." He shot a quick glance at his fellow officers, who grumbled agreement and went back to their work. "Besides," Tate added as he bent down to rub Chance's ears, "you brought along a snow rescue dog."

She gave him a grateful smile as Chance thumped his tail.

Tate stood again, looking more serious. "You should come with me, though." He headed through the station, toward the back, where she'd never been.

"I was actually hoping to talk to Peter," Alanna said, as she and Chance hurried after him. "I wanted to say goodbye."

"There's someone who wants to talk to you first." He gestured to the closed conference room door ahead of him.

Was Darcy in there? Had she agreed to talk to her after all? But why? And why would the police agree to it?

Or maybe it was the kids? Or their parents, wanting to know how to help them recover from the trauma of being kidnapped?

Even though it was part of what she did for a living, this was too personal. She was still too conflicted to offer the support they needed.

She shook her head, backed up a step, but then Tate pushed the door open for her.

On the other side of it, the police chief and Peter glanced her way. Then Kensie and Colter were there, hugging her, almost squashing baby Elysia between them.

Yet again, Kensie had flown across the country for her. This time, she'd brought her husband, five-month-old baby and their dog, too. She'd always been willing to do anything to protect Alanna. From the moment she'd wrapped her in a hug in Luna's hospital five years ago, Alanna had discovered her big sister always seemed to know exactly what she needed.

Rebel and Chance barked greetings to each other as Alanna breathed, "What are you doing here?"

"What are *you* doing here, sis?" Kensie asked her with a troubled gaze as she leaned back. "Why didn't you call us? We'd have come with you."

Peter looked at the police chief and said, "Let's give them have some privacy." The chief nodded and they left the room, keeping the door ajar.

In a quick burst, Alanna gave her sister and brother-in-law the short, ugly version of what had happened with Darcy.

Kensie stared at her a long moment, then asked, "What about the cop?" She nodded toward Peter in the other room.

Alanna glanced at him and blurted, "I owe him an

apology." Kensie and her husband shared a smile over her head.

Then Colter announced, "Kensie and I came here to bring you home, Alanna. But I think we're going to spend the night at my cabin. We haven't been there in more than a year. I want to show the place to Miss Elysia here." He took his daughter from Kensie, bounced her in his arms and mumbled baby talk to her, then added, "It'll give you time to make that apology."

"But—" Alanna gestured to Peter, staring at her from beyond the conference room with his usual intensity, and Kensie took her hand.

"This time, when you come home, I don't want you to have any regrets, Alanna."

"I didn't—"

"It wasn't fair of us to think you'd want to leave this whole life behind, just walk away from everyone."

"You didn't," Alanna interrupted. "You encouraged me to stay in touch with Sydney and Johnny. You tried to help convince Drew's and Valerie's parents to let me talk to them. You've always supported me."

"But I should have understood how hard it was for you to leave the people who'd raised you, too," Kensie said. When Alanna tried to protest again, she pressed on. "You did a good thing, coming here to help find those kids. I know you're upset about how it all went down, but that's not your fault. And I can see that you found something else while you were here."

Alanna flushed and tried not to glance at Peter as Kensie winked and added, "Big sisters always know."

"It's not what you think," Alanna tried to explain.

Her connection with Peter was forged from a situation that had ended. It would break as soon as she stepped on that plane.

"Maybe, maybe not," Kensie said, finality in her voice, a big sister tone Alanna had always secretly loved. "But years later, I don't want you thinking 'I should have, could have...' So, Colter is right."

"Happens sometimes," Colter interjected, making faces at Elysia as she squirmed and giggled.

Kensie rolled her eyes at her husband, then hugged Alanna once more. "Don't do it here. Go see him after work. Talk. Just be honest and at least then, whatever happens, you can move forward. Okay?"

Alanna nodded, unable to stop herself from glancing at Peter, who'd been staring at her as if he knew he was the subject of their conversation.

ALANNA STARED AT the house in front of her, at the light shining through the curtains, the shadow moving inside. Her engine was still running as she debated whether she could go through with it.

Alanna could hear her sister's voice in her head from this morning, telling her she needed closure.

She'd never be able to have closure with Julian. The same was probably true of Darcy now, as well. It was too late to change either of those things. But she could find closure with Peter.

It had seemed like a good idea to go to Peter's house when Kensie had suggested it this morning. But ten hours later, she was having doubts.

Woof! Woof!

Chance's bark startled her and made the curtains part in the house's window.

"*Chance*," she chided as Peter stepped outside, wearing just jeans and a long-sleeved T-shirt in the frigid weather.

Alanna turned off the engine and got out of her car, an apology already on her lips as Chance leaped out after her.

"Come on," Peter said, cutting off her apology and turning back for the house, his expression inscrutable. "It's cold out here."

Chance bounded up alongside him, accepting Peter's ruffling of the fur on his head before he jumped up the stairs and into the house.

Alanna followed a little more slowly, nerves building.

When she stepped inside, he helped her out of her thick winter coat, silent but not taking his gaze from hers. This singular focus made her flush and then he smiled.

His default expression was always so serious: his lips pressed together, his gaze steady, the sharp lines of his face making him seem even more intense. His was the face of a police officer. But his smile was a little bit crooked, a little bit shy. It made him seem younger, more approachable. It charmed her.

When he smiled, she could imagine walking beside him, tentatively slipping her hand into his. She could envision the giddy nervousness of a first date, the sweetness of a first kiss and then the smile on his face giving way to a thrilling intensity as he lay with her in front of the fireplace.

Awareness flickered in his eyes, then he stepped back, giving her more space than she wanted. "Let's sit by the fire." He headed that way, tapping his leg, calling, "You, too, Chance."

Her St. Bernard hurried after Peter, tail wagging. When Peter sat on the couch, Chance lay at his feet.

Alanna settled awkwardly a few feet away, angled toward him. She twisted her hands together, trying to remember the words she'd planned out on the drive to his house. But they wouldn't come and she turned away, her attention snagging on the bare wall across from her.

"You took down the pictures," she said.

"It's going to make my family happy. They're going to ask what prompted such a big change." His hand skimmed hers, then he shifted closer until they were sharing a seat. "I've been focusing on the wrong things. You taught me that."

"What? I did? How?"

The smile was back, amused now, less self-conscious. But those bright blue eyes were still laser-locked on hers, practically hypnotic. "You've had to make a lot of hard choices. Pretty much everyone around you—all these people who love you—they expect something from you. I see you trying to do right by all of them. I see you putting your own needs last. And honestly, with all the reasons you have to hate some of the people involved, you always seem to choose love."

Alanna shook her head, blew out the breath she'd been holding. Was that really how he saw her? She wished it were true. "I try to be fair to everyone, but it doesn't always work. It feels like I let people down a lot."

"You don't—"

"I let you down," she interrupted, flipping her hand over to squeeze his, trying not to fixate on how perfectly his hand seemed to fit with hers. "I owe you an apology. I shouldn't have run off without telling you where I was going. I shouldn't have forced you to make a decision that would hurt your career."

"I made my choice," he said, confirming what she'd suspected—his career as a police officer was in danger. "And I'd do it again." He lifted her hand, his breath dancing over her skin as he whispered, "If only we didn't live across the country…" Then he pressed his lips to her knuckles.

It was the briefest touch, but it made her skin tingle and her whole body warm.

"I wish…" Her voice came out so soft she wondered if he could even hear it.

He shifted even closer, pressed against her from knee to shoulder. "What?"

When she'd lived in Desparre, she'd been sheltered, isolated. She'd barely had the opportunity to talk to people outside of her own home. She'd certainly never dated.

When she'd returned to Chicago, Kensie had encouraged her to get out, meet people, join activities. She'd dated sporadically, but it had always felt awkward, tinged with a voyeuristic curiosity about her kidnapping on their part. She'd never developed a real connection with any of them.

Sitting next to Peter felt natural. It felt like she was supposed to be here. And now she was leaving again.

She didn't realize a tear had spilled from one eye until Peter swiped it away. His warm hand stayed on her face, turning to cup her cheek, stroke down the length of her neck. All the while, he never took his eyes from hers.

She couldn't seem to get a full breath as he leaned closer, so slowly, and his lips finally grazed hers. Then suddenly her free hand was clutching the front of his T-shirt and the fingers he had been resting on her collarbone moved into her hair. He took her upper lip between his, brushed his tongue against the seam of her mouth.

Pulling him toward her, she wrapped her arms around his back and held on tight, leaning into his kiss, demanding more. She didn't want to think about tomorrow, didn't want to think about leaving. She only wanted Peter, for as long as they had together.

He groaned, the sound somewhere between frustration and need, and then she was in a controlled fall until her back hit the couch cushions, her feet still dangling on the floor. Peter angled over her, his weight on his elbows as his lips met hers again, his kisses still unhurried even as she arched up toward him.

She slid her hands down his back, pulling him toward her, thrilling in the sudden contact as he lowered his weight more fully onto her, as she shifted so her whole body was underneath him. Running her hands through his hair, over his shoulders, she fused her lips to his. The world around her seemed to fade away until all she could think of, all she could feel, was *Peter*.

The phone vibrating in her pocket startled her, made her jerk. She yanked it out of her pocket, ready to toss it on the floor, when she saw the name on the caller ID. Kensie knew she'd come here tonight, probably knew she wouldn't want any interruptions. So why was she calling now?

As she squirmed to sit up, Peter moved off of her but stroked her hand.

Her voice was breathless as she answered, "Hello?" She cringed at how she sounded.

"Alanna?" Kensie's panicked voice made Alanna's head clear fast.

"What's wrong?"

Her older sister, who'd risked her life to find Alanna five years ago and come to her aid once again, burst into tears. "She's gone!" Her words were garbled over the tears as she rushed on. "Someone came into the cabin. Elysia was sleeping. Now, she's just gone. Alanna, she's been kidnapped!"

Chapter Fifteen

"How is this possible?" Alanna paced in front of the fire, her skin still flushed from their embrace, her lips still slightly swollen from his kisses. With panic all over her face, she spun to face him. "How?"

"I don't know." Peter stood, used his free hand to pull her against his chest as he listened to the officer on the other end of the phone. "Are you sure?" he asked the officer, then swore.

"Well?" Alanna demanded.

Peter shook his head. "Darcy is still behind bars. They just confirmed it. She didn't escape again."

"And?"

"And nothing. She's not saying a word."

Alanna hurried across the room and picked up her coat, fumbling as she tried to get it on. Chance raced after her, barked once, then looked back at Peter.

He followed and grabbed the coat out of her hand. "Just hold on, okay? Let's not waste time driving around. Let's figure out what's going on here."

"This can't be a coincidence," Alanna said, her voice too high-pitched, panic in every shaky movement.

"I know." He pulled her back into his arms, held on tight. "I know. We'll find her."

He felt tension all through her body and wished he could rewind to five minutes ago, before Elysia had been abducted out of the Hayeses' cabin a mere twenty feet from her sleeping parents. Back to Alanna breathless and kissing him, back to a time when nothing else mattered.

He'd been expecting her at his doorstep, had known an apology was coming. He'd planned to cut it off to let her know how she'd impacted his life. He hadn't planned to tell her that he'd developed complicated feelings for her. He definitely hadn't expected anything to happen between them.

Now none of it could matter. Because somehow, from behind bars, Darcy Altier had orchestrated the abduction of Alanna's niece. "It could be a copycat," he theorized out loud. Maybe Darcy's media attention had spurred someone else into action.

"Really? Another kidnapper?" Alanna squirmed free of his tight hold just enough to look up at him from within the circle of his arms, her expression skeptical.

She was only a few inches shorter than him, and he was tempted to lean down slightly and kiss her forehead. He ignored the urge and agreed with her. "Probably not. But Julian is dead. Darcy's been in jail for five years. How likely is it that she managed to find a new partner while she was on her way here from Oregon?"

"There's no way," Alanna said, pulling away from him and starting to pace again, her hands curled into fists. "Maybe Darcy paid someone? I mean, it's Elysia."

Her voice cracked and she swiped a hand over her eyes. "Darcy is trying to hurt me because I turned her in five years ago, because I came after her again. I should have stayed home. I should have made sure Kensie stayed home. I can't believe Darcy would do this! I can't believe—"

Peter pulled her back against him just as Chance ran over and pressed against her side, nudging her with his big head. "It's not your fault."

"Of course it's my fault!"

"Alanna—"

"Let's not argue about this." She spun in his arms to face him, staring up at him with desperation and trust. A trust he probably hadn't earned. "Let's just figure out how to find my niece."

"We will," he promised, praying he could keep his word.

To find Elysia, he had to figure out if Darcy had contacted someone. Who would help her? According to the station, Darcy hadn't made a single call since she'd been arrested yesterday. Maybe someone had acted without her needing to ask? Maybe they'd seen the news and taken their own revenge.

But who?

"Could it be someone she met in jail back in Oregon?" he asked. It was an odd thing to consider, but it definitely happened.

"Wouldn't that person still be in jail?" Alanna was obviously not following his trail of thinking.

"I mean, someone who visited her. You know those women who marry men on death row? Or marry murderers while they're still in jail, then move in with them when they get released? It happens with female inmates and male civilians, too."

Alanna shook her head. "Darcy was already married. Julian—"

"Was in jail, too. They were separated, in two different prisons. Maybe someone started visiting her. Even if she wasn't interested, maybe they followed the news. They could have followed her here. Maybe it was their way of trying to win her over. Stranger things have happened."

Alanna looked skeptical, but it was the best idea he had. It made a lot more sense if it was someone who'd visited Darcy, who'd schemed with her. Someone whose trust she'd earned, someone who'd do anything to make her happy.

No matter what Alanna thought about Darcy and Julian's relationship, these were people who'd spent nearly two decades with kids they'd kidnapped. They were both capable of manipulation. Maybe someone desperate and lonely had visited Darcy in prison and she'd seen an opportunity. Then, when she'd managed to escape, he'd followed her here and taken revenge when she'd gone back to jail.

That actually seemed possible. No matter what Peter thought of Darcy's actions, he'd seen the love for Alanna in her eyes. He could absolutely picture her kidnapping kids she didn't know, trying to re-create what she and Julian had once had. But he wasn't sure he could imagine her intentionally hurting Alanna by having her niece kidnapped by someone else.

It wasn't her MO. Whatever messed up psychology had allowed her to rationalize kidnapping children, she'd grabbed them with the intent of raising them. This was different. Elysia's kidnapping seemed malicious, angry, driven by revenge.

"I'm going to talk to the US Marshals she got away from back in Oregon," he told Alanna. "They've probably already looked into who visited her in prison. Hopefully they'll share that info with me. Otherwise, I'll try the prison."

Pulling out his phone again, he looked up the number for one of the US marshals who'd accompanied Darcy to Julian's burial. He'd spoken to the agent a few days ago to give her a heads-up that he thought Darcy could be in Alaska. At the time, she'd seemed overworked and overstressed and seriously doubtful that Darcy had made it so far north so fast.

When she picked up now and he explained the situation, there was a long pause. Then she admitted, "We can't be sure about this, but it's possible Darcy had help escaping us at Julian's burial."

Peter swallowed back words of frustration that he hadn't heard about this the first time he'd called. "Who?"

"We don't know. We don't even know if he was in on it. At the time, we assumed it was a coincidence. But given what you're telling me now, maybe we should have looked at it more closely. The distraction he caused, right when he caused it… He left right after, with the rest of the crowd. We never tracked him down."

"It's what gave Darcy a chance to run?" Peter

guessed, as Alanna tilted her head close to his, listening in.

"Yeah."

"You have a description?"

"It was a man. Younger than her. Probably white."

Peter let out a noise that sounded like a laugh, but was all frustration. "That's it?"

"It was drizzling. He was wearing a dark raincoat. He wasn't particularly close to us and he wasn't our priority. There was a big crowd there, gawkers and press, plus mourners from another burial service nearby. He was in the wind immediately."

"Okay." Peter sighed, then said, "A little girl is missing. We think it's connected to Darcy. Do you know *anything* else about this guy that could help?"

"I'm sorry."

"Did you look into who visited her in prison?"

"Of course. But no one visited her. We confirmed with the prison that she received mail, but following procedure, they didn't read it. And whatever she received wasn't in her cell after her escape."

"What about phone calls?"

"Nope. She requested to have all the kids she abducted on her approved contact list, if you can believe it, but obviously, that was denied."

"Thanks." When he hung up, he saw how tightly Alanna's lips were pursed together, how her eyes were twitching like she was holding back tears. "I'm going to call my department. Whoever Darcy is working with, she had to contact that person somehow. If it was via mail, maybe one of her cell mates knows who was writing her. We'll find him. In the meantime, let's—"

The buzzing of his phone cut him off. He answered and told his partner, "Tate, I was just about to call you. Alanna's niece—"

"Has been kidnapped. Colter Hayes called us twenty minutes ago. You need to get in to the station right now."

"We're trying to run down leads," Peter told him, squeezing the hand Alanna had placed in his, watching her wipe away tears. "I think—"

"I've got a lead. I need you here right now," Tate interrupted, then hung up.

THE MOON WAS an ominous sliver in an angry gray sky when Peter whipped his truck into the Desparre PD parking lot.

Alanna leaped out as he put the vehicle in Park, Chance chasing after her. She raced across the lot to the station's door, sliding on a patch of ice and pinwheeling her arms until she regained her balance. Her frustration at the lack of information had grown unbearable on the way over. All Peter had told her after hanging up with Tate was that there was a lead.

Peter didn't live that far from the station—less than ten minutes at the near-dangerous speeds he'd been driving. But she'd felt every one of those minutes like they were hours. Elysia was out there somewhere, at the mercy of a stranger.

Alanna had never felt a joy quite like the day she'd gone to the hospital to meet her niece. She'd spent years agonizing over her choice to leave behind "siblings" she'd loved, so she could return to siblings she'd missed but who'd become vague memories. But that first moment she'd held Elysia in her arms, she'd been so overcome with love, she'd nearly burst into tears. That moment had been worth every doubt, every ounce of guilt she'd tried to psychoanalyze away.

Now Elysia was in danger. And it was because of her.

Yanking the door to the police station open, Alanna nearly stumbled as Chance raced in past her, barking a greeting that was returned immediately. Rebel was here. Which meant Kensie and Colter were, too.

The door marked Police Only was propped open and Chance bolted through it. Even though she knew Kensie and Colter would never blame her, Alanna's steps faltered. Her anxiety ratcheted up, but then Kensie was running toward her. Colter hurried after his wife, his gait uneven as he leaned on the cane he rarely used, his wartime injury obviously acting up. Before Peter had even finished slipping through the door behind her, Kensie and Colter had their arms around Alanna, a family hug that reminded her how much she'd missed in all her years away. Chance doubled back, running circles around Colter and Kensie's Malinois-German Shepherd, until the two of them pushed their way into the circle.

A short burst of anxious laughter broke through her threatening tears as Alanna pulled out of the tight embrace. She saw the panic and desperation on Kensie and Colter's faces and a sob burst free. "I'm sorry."

"Don't," Colter snapped, something deadly coming into his eyes that might have been his war face.

"It's not your fault. We need to focus on getting her back, not on regrets."

Alanna nodded, swiping away the tears that had spilled despite her best efforts. "What do we know?"

At the question, Tate appeared, frowning as his eyes skimmed down the top page in a big stack of paper. "Not what we expected."

"What does that mean?" Alanna demanded, tired of all the cryptic information.

"Let's go sit in the conference room." Tate nodded briefly at Peter, then spun back the way he'd come.

Alanna hurried after him, alongside her sister, brother-in-law, Peter and the two dogs. Together, they all crammed into the little conference room and then Tate announced, "The parents of those two kidnapped kids arrived late this evening." He glanced at his watch and then amended his statement. "Technically, yesterday. Once they saw their kids, we sat down and talked to them about what happened."

"I'm sorry," Kensie interrupted, her hand clutched tight in her husband's, her eyes and nose bright red like she'd been crying fiercely not long ago. "What does this have to do with Elysia? Do you have any leads on where she is?"

Tate set the stack of papers on the table, rubbed the side of his hand against his forehead like he was exhausted. "We all assumed Darcy had kidnapped those kids."

"What?" The floor seemed to move underneath her and Alanna flung her hand out to steady herself on something. Before she could grip anything, Peter was holding her arm, keeping her upright.

"She *did* kidnap them, didn't she?" She looked from Tate to Peter and back again. "She had those kids at the cabin…" Or did she? They'd obviously been at the second cabin, but at the first one, Alanna had only seen her run out the door. Where were the kids then?

"It sounds like she was involved," Tate said, "but…" He glanced at them, leaning against the wall, holding onto each other, the dogs positioned in front as if standing guard. "Why don't you all sit?"

"Just tell us," Colter demanded, his arm tight around Kensie's shoulders. "What's going on?"

"According to the kids, Darcy didn't grab either of them. The little boy said it was a man, much younger than Darcy, who kidnapped them and brought them back to Darcy."

"I've been in touch with the Marshals who were watching her in Oregon," Peter jumped in. "It sounds like this could be the same person who helped her escape at the burial. We need to talk to the prison, try and see if we can figure out who was writing her there. She must have met someone through letters, convinced him to help her escape."

Was that really what had happened? Or was the answer much simpler? Alanna felt herself sway as Tate continued.

"Apparently, when you caught up to Darcy and the kids at the second cabin, this man was out. When you found her at the first one, he'd already taken the kids to the second location. Both times, he had their vehicle.

Darcy had needed to start that avalanche so she could slip away and wait somewhere for this guy to pick her up. It's why she didn't have anywhere to go at the second cabin. Darcy was supposed to erase all traces of them and then call to get picked up again."

"Did they mention a name? Have we pressed Darcy on who it is?" Peter asked. "Or I can call the prison right now, light a fire under them, so that they—"

"You don't need to do that," Alanna said. "I know who it is." She looked at Kensie and Colter, shaking her head in disbelief, ashamed that it hadn't occurred to her before now that Darcy might have had help.

Darcy might see a child from a distance that she wanted, that she believed should have been her child. But it had always been Julian who'd made it happen. With Julian out of the picture, there was only one person Alanna could think of who would try to piece together a new family for Darcy.

"It was my older 'brother,' Johnny."

Chapter Sixteen

"Johnny is the kidnapper," Tate confirmed. When Kensie gasped and looked to Alanna, Tate said, "We don't have a recent photo of Johnny, but we showed the kids a picture from when he was rescued five years ago and they confirmed it was him."

"Why?" Kensie asked Alanna. She was flushed with panic and clutching Colter, whose expression had morphed into a fury Alanna had never seen before. "Why would he kidnap those kids? And why would he take Elysia?"

"He's—" Alanna choked on a sob, then took a deep breath to get control of herself. Focusing on all the mistakes she'd made, worrying about all the worst-case scenarios for her niece wasn't going to help right now. She needed to focus on what had happened to turn Johnny into a kidnapper. Maybe that would help them figure out where he was now and how to stop him.

"He was the first one the Altiers kidnapped," Alanna said, trying to work it out in her mind at the same time she tried to explain to everyone else. "He was five years old. As we grew up, he remembered his family, but barely."

"He refused to talk to you once you came to Chicago. He…" Lines appeared between Kensie's eyebrows as she squinted into the distance, into a memory. "He's the one who shot at me and Colter at the cabin five years ago, isn't he? That was him with the gun?"

Alanna nodded, wishing she could make it untrue. Wishing she could have gotten through to Darcy enough to get her to admit that Johnny was involved.

"He won't hurt Elysia," she blurted. Whatever Johnny had become, he'd never harm a child. Right now it felt like the only thing in her life she knew for certain.

"Alanna," Colter said, judgment and barely contained anger in his voice. "I know he was your big brother for a long time, but—"

"I'm not trying to make excuses for him." She cut Colter off, even though the thought of Johnny doing any of this made her chest hurt so bad she wanted to double over. He might not be her blood, but he *was* still her big brother. When she'd first been kidnapped, feeling terrified and alone, he had comforted her. He'd promised to always look out for her, look after her. He'd said they were brother and sister now and that would never change.

Except if he'd kidnapped Elysia, it *had* changed. There was nothing random about it. While the idea of Darcy grabbing Alanna's niece for revenge had seemed out of character, Alanna could imagine Johnny doing it far too easily.

The truth was, everything between them had changed

five years ago. From the moment she'd left that note and brought the scrutiny of the FBI, Johnny's brotherly love had turned into confusion and then hate. When Kensie and Colter had tried to rescue her, Johnny had seen Darcy pick up a weapon, so he'd done the same. He hadn't spoken to her since that moment when the Altiers had been arrested, and he'd barely spoken to the rest of their "siblings," either.

"Drew's and Valerie's parents won't let them talk to any of us. Johnny won't talk to me, so he's only been in contact with Sydney since that day. Sydney said…"

Alanna frowned, wishing she'd tried harder to reach out to Johnny, found a way to get through to him. But every phone call had gone unanswered. Even her emails and letters had never gotten a response. Over the years, she'd all but stopped trying, reducing her attempts to a few letters a year she knew he'd never read.

If she hadn't given up on him, would it have come to this?

"*What*?" Kensie pushed, tears and anger mixing in her voice.

Alanna tried to focus. "Sydney said Johnny moved back to Alaska. When his birth family came to get him, he was already twenty-three. Initially, he went home with them to Colorado, but apparently it never felt like home to him. The last time Sydney and I talked about Johnny, she said he barely spoke to his birth family anymore. I think they gave up trying to build a relationship with him, because he didn't want one."

For Johnny, the Altiers had become his only family. When she'd left the note to tell the world she was still alive, she'd destroyed that family. From then on, he'd essentially been all alone.

"So this kid—man, since he's twenty-eight now— learned Julian had been killed. He was devastated, but saw it as his opportunity to help Darcy escape," Peter said, thinking quickly. "He went to Oregon for the burial, but also to create a distraction and help Darcy get free. They traveled to Alaska together and presumably hatched a plan to kidnap kids along the way. Or maybe they planned the kidnappings before that, when he wrote to her in prison, as soon as they learned Darcy was granted furlough for the burial."

"I think the recent kidnappings were spur-of-the-moment," Alanna said, remembering how Darcy had spoken of seeing her as a child and just *knowing*. She pictured those two kids in the cabin, so similar to the way she and Johnny had once looked. "I think Darcy saw a kid and felt a connection, felt like the child should have been hers. Then Johnny made it happen, like Julian used to do."

She flushed, realizing the one piece of information she'd held back five years ago suddenly mattered now. "Johnny knew how to do it because..." She squeezed her eyes shut, hating that her "brother" had been involved at all, wondering if he'd ever really had a chance to return to a normal life. Wishing she'd tried harder to help him.

"Why?" Colter asked, stepping closer. His dog, Rebel, who'd been in war zones with him as a Combat Tracker Dog, stuck close to his side, knowing when Colter needed him.

"When they kidnapped me and Johnny, they saw an

opportunity and took it. But with all the other kids, they *created* opportunities. Darcy and Julian saw Sydney at a playground and they had Johnny lure her around a corner from where her parents were sitting, so they could grab her."

"*What*?" Kensie blurted, looking horrified but also distrustful, as if she wondered what else Alanna had kept from her. "You never told me that."

"It wasn't in the police reports, either," Tate said, his narrowed gaze on her.

To his credit, Peter kept holding her hand. She was afraid to look at his expression as she tried to explain. "Johnny was only thirteen when that happened. Did he really have a choice? I didn't want Johnny to get in trouble because he did what the people he'd called his parents since he was five told him to do. I didn't want him to get charged."

"He was a minor," Peter said softly. "He wouldn't have been charged." When she looked at him, her misery probably clear in her eyes, he asked, "That's not all he did, is it? What about Valerie and Drew?"

She could feel all eyes on her again, and she forced herself to look at Kensie and Colter. "For those abductions, Julian asked Johnny to distract the parents, pretend he needed help while Julian grabbed the kids." She ducked her head as Kensie and Colter stared back at her, disappointment and disbelief all over their faces. "I didn't know about it until after the fact," she added as if it mattered.

Ultimately, when she'd known anything related to kidnappings didn't really matter, did it? It's what Peter had been getting at the first time he'd met her. Yes, she'd been a kid, but she'd had fourteen long years when she could have spoken up, when she could have stopped this.

"He was older then," Tate said when she went quiet. "He would have been seventeen with Drew and twenty-one with Valerie. An adult."

"Yes," Alanna admitted. "But he was a victim, too. They took him when he was five years old and raised him with love, but also raised him to be theirs. He reacted to it differently than the rest of us, maybe because when they kidnapped him, he didn't have anyone to reassure him, like the rest of us did." It had been *Johnny* who'd first gotten through to her, comforted her, made her feel safe when her whole world was turned upside down. He'd done the same for Sydney, Drew and Valerie.

"None of this was ever his choice. Drew and Valerie, they didn't remember their families, but the rest of us—we felt torn between these lives we sort of remembered and the life we had, the family who loved us." She swiped more tears away, begging Kensie to understand. "I'm so sorry. If I'd ever thought—"

"You were trying to protect someone you loved. I understand why you didn't tell." Kensie's voice sounded understanding, but her hands were fisted, betrayal in the depths of her eyes.

"I'm so sorry," Alanna repeated, but it felt like she was talking into a void, like it was already far too late. She'd tried so hard to do right by everyone and in the end, maybe she'd done right by no one.

Peter squeezed her hand, but she didn't look at him, didn't want to see the judgment there, too.

"So, what's the dynamic *now*?" Tate asked when the silence dragged on too long. "Who's in charge? Darcy? Now that she's behind bars again, Johnny is after revenge, right?" His gaze skipped to Colter and Kensie and he grimaced as he looked back at her. "What does that mean for Elysia? You said he'd never hurt her, didn't you? So what's his endgame?"

Alanna looked around the room, at four pairs of eyes all staring at her, waiting for an answer. It was an answer she didn't have.

HE'D BEEN RIGHT from the beginning.

Peter stared at Alanna, who was trying so hard to hold it together, and remembered the distrust and suspicion he'd felt when he'd realized who she was. Had that only been six days ago?

Despite everything that had happened since then, he'd been right. He just hadn't been right about Alanna.

When this all started, he would have felt vindicated that his theory wasn't illogical. He'd believed from the very beginning that the kidnapper could be someone who'd been kidnapped and raised by the Altiers, who'd bonded so closely to them, he was now willing to do whatever it took to protect them. It wasn't unusual. Feigning loyalty to stay safe in the beginning could easily shift over time into a warped need to protect the very people who'd kidnapped you. But Alanna hadn't been the one afflicted. Her "brother" had been.

Alanna remembered Johnny as a vulnerable and confused boy, and it was messing with her perception. Peter saw the truth: Johnny was dangerous to them all.

Peter should have felt sorry for him, but instead, it took him back to that war zone, covered in blood and sand and knowing everything he'd worked for as a reporter was over in an instant. He could feel his hand twitching, a strong desire to touch his bad ear. Ignoring it, he tried to focus on what he'd just learned and what it meant for the investigation.

Johnny had been the one kidnapping kids all along. Regardless of Darcy's involvement—which was identifying a kid she wanted—Johnny had actually taken action. What else was he capable of? And how far would he go to get back at Alanna for what he perceived as the ways she'd done him wrong?

He squeezed Alanna's hand tighter, not wanting her to get close enough to Johnny to ever find out.

Across the room, Tate's gaze dropped to their linked hands, then up to Peter's face. Tate's lips pursed slightly—assessing or judging, Peter couldn't be sure. Right now, as much as he liked his partner and valued his opinion, Peter didn't really care. His job was already in jeopardy. The fact that they'd called him at all, that they were letting him in on the investigation, probably had more to do with his proximity to Alanna than their belief in him as an officer.

After the debacle at the cabin, the chief had told him to take a few days off. He'd only been at the station yesterday because the chief had called him in to give him a serious dressing-down. He was lucky she hadn't immediately demanded he hand over his badge and gun. But he knew that wasn't the end of it. She'd all but told him she was still deciding if he had a future on the force.

He had a reckoning coming at the Desparre PD. He didn't want to think about it, couldn't afford the distraction of worrying what it meant for his future, for the very way he'd come to identify himself. Right now, his sole focus had to be on finding Alanna's niece. And on keeping Alanna safe in the process.

It was his job, but it had become more than that. Whatever his connection to Alanna meant, however long it was destined to last, he couldn't let her down now. Not with so much of her happiness at stake. Because if her niece *wasn't* okay, Alanna would never be okay again, either.

"What do you think Johnny was trying to do?" he asked Alanna, tugging on her hand until she turned to face him, forcing her to shut out the stress of her family's reactions and focus on what she knew about her so-called brother. "When he was grabbing those kids Darcy pointed out, are you sure that's how it happened?"

Alanna squinted at him questioningly, her free hand absently stroking Chance's fur. Her loyal dog scooted closer, lending support, as she asked, "What do you mean?"

"Didn't you say that you decided to reach out with that note five years ago because Johnny had met someone, started talking about getting married? Is there any chance he was grabbing these kids for himself, that maybe Darcy being there just gave him the courage to do it? What about this woman he wanted to marry? Who was she?"

Alanna shrugged. "I barely remember her. Darcy and Julian trusted Johnny more than the rest of us, gave him more freedom because they said he'd earned it. He met a woman when he was in town and thought it was love at first sight. Darcy and Julian were skeptical and warned him about keeping the family's secrets, but he started dating her. Once the truth came out and our faces were all over the papers, she wanted nothing to do with him."

"So, you don't think he's trying to build his own family? That grabbing Elysia was just a way to do it and get revenge at the same time?" It might be the best option, the version of events that made it most likely Johnny would take care of Elysia rather than kill her.

"No." Alanna's near-tears of a few minutes ago had turned into something hard and determined. "I think he wanted to re-create the family he had."

"But that was never going to happen," Peter said.

"No. He won't talk to me. Drew's and Valerie's parents won't let him talk to them—and from what I've heard in news reports, they're always watched over. That just leaves Sydney. She talks to him every few months, but growing up, she was the one who remembered her birth family best. The Altiers grabbed her when she was six—older than the rest of us were when we were kidnapped. She's the one that Darcy and Julian always worried would say something and put the 'family' in danger. Besides, she's twenty-one now. She's going to college. She has her own life. It's pretty different from our isolated existence in Desparre. She told me more than once that she'd never come back here. I'm sure she said the same to Johnny."

"So, he decided to find new siblings?" Tate asked, getting Alanna back on track.

"That'd be my guess."

"And then you showed up," Tate said. "You ruined his plan, so he snatched Elysia."

Peter frowned, wondering if his partner was right. Maybe it was enough for Johnny to know Alanna was suffering. But his gut told him otherwise. Everything Alanna had said about Johnny suggested he'd been deeply damaged by his experience growing up, that he had the psychology of someone who would misdirect all their anger and rage at the easiest available target. What good was rage like that if the target didn't know who was hurting her?

Peter looked at Colter and Kensie. "Did you see Johnny at the cabin? Did he leave any indication that it was him? Some kind of message for Alanna?"

"Elysia was in her crib in the back room," Colter said. "Kensie and I had fallen asleep by the fire. We woke up because Rebel was going wild, trying to get into the bedroom. She might technically be a senior dog, but she still thinks like she's military. We ran back there and found it was locked. I was scared to kick the door in with Elysia in there, so I ran around outside. I found the window open." His jaw tightened, his lips turning inward. "Our daughter was gone."

"You didn't see anything? Not in the backyard or in the room? No note?" Tate pressed.

"If we had, don't you think we would have told you by now?" Colter snapped. He ran a hand through his dark blond hair, making it stick up. "Sorry. My daughter is five months old. We've just—" He choked on a sob, then finished, "I'm trying to hold it together here, but we have to find her."

Tate nodded, his expression saying he'd been in this room before with scared parents. He looked back at Alanna, and Peter was suddenly glad of Tate's extra years on the force, of his background as a police officer in a bigger city before he'd come to Desparre. "Are we waiting for a ransom note here, Alanna?"

Alanna shook her head, frustration and exhaustion on her face. "I don't know." Then that frustration morphed into angry determination. "But I know who does. I want to talk to Darcy."

Chapter Seventeen

"I don't understand you at all," Darcy said, staring at her from across the table inside the Desparre PD's claustrophobic interrogation room.

Tate and Peter had brought Alanna here, insisted that Darcy had to remain cuffed and then left them alone to talk. Of course, *alone* was a relative term. Alanna's gaze darted to the camera mounted in the corner. Whatever was said in here, Peter and Tate were watching. She didn't know who else from the department was with them.

Darcy looked even worse than she had at the cabin. Her shoulders were slumped inward and the lines pulling at the edges of her mouth and eyes seemed even more pronounced.

"I'm not sure I understand you, either," Alanna said, clutching her hands tightly together underneath the table, trying to keep her tone even, keep the anger and blame out of her voice. Darcy knew her better than most people on the planet; it was unlikely she'd be fooled.

"You let me go at the cabin," Darcy said, real confusion in her eyes. "You stood in front of me, gave me an opportunity to escape."

Alanna tensed, resisted the urge to glance at the camera surely recording every word spoken in this room. That hadn't been her reasoning at all, but she clamped her lips together, let Darcy continue. She'd rather fight an accomplice charge than risk angering Darcy, risk losing the chance to find out where Johnny had taken Elysia.

"So, why did you bring police in the first place? Why did you turn us in all those years ago? It's like you're two different people, Alanna." A humorless smile flitted across her face, before morphing into a scowl. "I should have realized it sooner, I guess. You're torn between two worlds. I saw it over the years when you were growing up, this far off look you'd get on your face, like you were dreaming about the family you'd been born to, instead of the one you were meant to be a part of. I thought you'd grown out of it before you wrote that note. After all those years, we thought we could trust you."

This again? Alanna fought down her frustration. The guilt she'd seen in Darcy's gaze, in her words, when Alanna had told her how her kidnapping had affected the Morgans, already seemed forgotten. Right now, seeing Darcy wasn't about getting an apology. It wasn't about getting closure on her past. The fact was, she'd probably never fully have it. That was something she needed to manage. And it was something she *could* manage, with her degree in psychology and her job helping others overcome worse trauma.

What she *did* need was for Darcy to understand the

hurt she'd caused. She needed to understand the further hurt she'd cause if she let Elysia stay with Johnny. It was the only way Alanna had a shot at getting Darcy to choose Alanna's happiness over that of the man she still called her son, the man who still called her Mom.

Alanna folded her arms in front of her on the table, leaned in.

Before she could speak, Darcy asked softly, "What happened to your ring?"

Alanna's hands twitched, her wish to keep them hidden under the table too late. Darcy had given her a worn ruby ring when she was sixteen years old. It was a family heirloom Darcy had worn most of Alanna's childhood. Alanna hadn't taken it off for three years. It was the only thing she'd taken with her when she'd left Alaska besides the clothes she'd been wearing the day police had split apart the "family."

The Morgans had all stared curiously at it when they didn't think she would notice, but they waited for her open up to them at her own speed. She hadn't wanted to hurt them, hadn't wanted to admit that she missed Darcy and Julian, that the ring felt like her final connection to them. Instead she'd taken it off, placed it carefully at the bottom of a drawer and hadn't put it on since.

"It's safe," Alanna said. "I still have it." She slid her hands back under the table, tried to get the conversation back on track. "You thought you could trust me? Well, you said you loved me. You said you wanted to raise me to be strong and happy."

The offense was as obvious on Darcy's face as it was in her voice when she insisted, "I do. I did."

Alanna leaned toward her again, closing the space between them, letting Darcy see the hurt and fear on her face. "Then why would you let Johnny take my niece?"

Darcy's mouth dropped open into a small *O*. She shook her head slightly, her brow furrowed, but she didn't quite meet Alanna's gaze.

"You didn't know?" Alanna demanded, not sure if the confusion on Darcy's face was feigned or real. Hope started to replace the fear that talking to Darcy was too much of a long shot. If she really hadn't known, she'd be more likely to help Elysia. But would she be able to? Would she know how to get through to Johnny?

"I— No. That wasn't part of the plan. I didn't even know your niece was here. Heck, I didn't even know you *had* a niece. It's not like you talk to me anymore." She scowled, then gave a quick, hard shake of her head. Her voice was sad and lost when she continued, "We just wanted what we had before. We weren't trying to hurt you. We weren't trying to hurt anyone."

"But you know you did, right?" Alanna asked softly, willing Darcy to look at her, to face what she'd done. "Just like you knew what you'd done to all of our families. You tried not to think about it, tried to convince yourself the families you stole from would all be fine, that the kids you ripped away from them were happy. But deep down, you knew. You *knew* it was wrong."

Tears filled Darcy's eyes and she blinked rapidly, clearing them away. She started to reach her hand out, then looked at the cuffs keeping them locked together and faltered.

Alanna leaned farther across the table, closing her

hand over the top of Darcy's linked hands, hoping she wouldn't fixate on the missing ring again. Not that many years ago, Darcy's hands had been smooth and soft, deceivingly small for how strong she was. Those hands had picked Alanna up hundreds—thousands?— of times as a child. They'd sewn her clothes and helped her build a desk for her studies. They'd wiped away her tears and wrapped around her in loving hugs that Alanna still missed.

Now those same hands felt paper-thin, dry and rough. They looked older, too, as if she'd aged twenty years in prison instead of five.

The guilt that was never far beneath the surface bubbled up. Normally, Alanna reminded herself that she had no reason to feel guilty, that she'd done the right thing. This time, she let Darcy see all of her conflicted emotions, hoped it would help Darcy admit to some of her own.

"Please," Alanna whispered. "Elysia is only five months old. Johnny doesn't know how to take care of a baby that young. Not alone. And my sister deserves to get her child back. Kensie has been through enough."

"I…" Darcy's cheek twitched, her lips twisting downward. Her gaze skipped away from Alanna.

"Johnny still has a chance to make a normal life for himself."

Was it true? Alanna didn't really know. Not only because he'd certainly be facing charges for helping a prisoner escape and kidnapping three children, but also because everything that had happened in the past week proved he was more damaged by their upbringing than Alanna had ever realized.

Still, there was one thing she knew for sure. Turning himself in, handing Elysia over unharmed, was the only chance he had.

Darcy looked up at her, eyes narrowed and unreadable.

"Please help me find them," Alanna begged, squeezing Darcy's hands under hers.

Darcy ripped her hands away and turned her gaze to the ground, but not before Alanna saw the regret there. "You're lying to me. I'm not going to help you relegate Johnny to the same life I've had, the life Julian had. I love my son."

She looked up at Alanna once more, finality in the hardness of her eyes, the clenched line of her jaw. "Goodbye, Alanna."

SHE'D FAILED.

Alanna stood outside the interrogation room, her whole body too heavy with dread to move. Even knowing that Peter and Tate had surely already seen everything over the camera feed, Alanna didn't want to face them. More than that, she didn't want to face Kensie and Colter, didn't want to have to admit that their best lead to find Elysia was gone.

The finality in Darcy's goodbye had brought tears to Alanna's eyes. Just as quickly, she'd blinked them away, vowing never to shed another tear over Darcy or Julian Altier.

Yes, they'd raised her with love. But ultimately, everything they'd done had been selfish.

Five years ago, Alanna thought she'd taken a huge step in regaining control over her own life. But maybe she'd just been living in limbo, stuck between two worlds, between two families.

Now, finally, she was picking sides. But she'd done it much too late.

Taking a deep breath to control her anxiety, wishing she had Chance beside her, Alanna forced herself to move back toward the station's bullpen, toward Kensie and Colter.

As soon as she rounded the corner, there they were, crowding around her, fear and hope in their eyes that quickly turned to disappointment when they saw Alanna's face.

Kensie swallowed hard and clutched her husband's hand. Then she reached for Alanna's hand, too, always the big sister, even when Alanna didn't deserve it. "We'll find another way," she croaked, but her voice was full of fear. "The police are already combing the woods around our cabin, looking for trails. They'll find something."

Chance, obviously sensing Alanna's distress, pushed his way through the crowd until he was beside her, his big head nudging her arm. Rebel hurried over, too, slipping in between, so she could press up against Colter and Kensie at the same time.

Alanna stroked her dog's fur, letting his calming presence relax her too-rapid heartbeat. She looked past her family to Peter and Tate, who were standing a few steps away.

Peter stared back at her with sympathy in his eyes, no obvious sign of the distrust he had to be feeling after all of the things Darcy had said about her. Beside him, Tate looked more pensive, but Alanna was surprised to see that he didn't seem angry or distrustful, either.

"What Darcy said—"

Peter stepped closer, cutting her off. "You did your best. I'm sorry she let you down."

She blinked back at him and for half a second, it felt like it was just the two of them in that station. She could see in his eyes that he understood, that he hadn't ever believed she was trying to let Darcy go. A smile trembled on her lips, remembering his frustration in that moment back in the cabin and knowing he'd chosen to believe her.

It faded just as fast as reality rushed back in. Elysia was still missing. Without Darcy's help, how would they find Johnny? Without Darcy's help, how did Johnny expect to care for a newborn while he was on the run?

"He never planned to," she realized aloud.

"What?" Kensie asked, leaning closer, probably recognizing the excitement in Alanna's voice.

"Without Darcy, Johnny's not trying to re-create a family anymore. He's looking for revenge."

Kensie and Colter shared a worried glance, maybe because they'd already decided Johnny had grabbed Elysia out of revenge. They were probably worried it meant Johnny saw Elysia as expendable.

It was more than simple revenge, though. Darcy was

all highs and lows, lots of excitement followed by periods of depression. But she always acted with love, even when it was misguided. And until now, she'd stood by all of her "children," no matter what. Johnny followed her lead when it came to his mood swings, but his emotions were always all or nothing. Love or hate. Once the pendulum swung, it was hard to send it back.

He'd treated her like his best friend growing up, the little sister he was so happy to have by his side no matter what. When she'd left that note, all that love had twisted into fury. There was no in-between for him.

If Johnny had given up on rebuilding a family, then his entire goal was revenge. It meant Tate had been right when he'd asked what use revenge was if she didn't know it was Johnny. But with the kids rescued, of course they'd eventually figure out it was him. What Johnny needed her to know now was how to find him. What he needed was a reason to make her come. He'd found the reason. And she knew where to go.

Johnny had returned to where it had all started. He was at their cabin in Desparre.

Chapter Eighteen

"Why are we out here?" Tate demanded, zipping his coat up to his chin.

Alanna looked around the circle of people she'd hustled out of the station and into the snow. Kensie and Colter had Rebel between them, and the dog looked as curious as her owners in the darkened parking lot. Peter stood beside her, absently petting Chance and waiting for her to speak, his narrowed eyes telling her he already suspected what was coming.

When she'd told them all she needed to go outside for some fresh air, she'd hoped Tate would stay inside. Some part of her had hoped Peter would, too. Because if either of them refused to go along with her plan, her niece could be in more danger.

"Maybe you should go in and warm up," Alanna suggested, trying to sound sincere.

"You figured out where they are, didn't you?" Tate demanded.

"What?" Kensie gasped, clutching her hand. "Really?"

Alanna stared back at the big sister who looked so much like her and nodded. "I think so. But…" Her gaze darted to Peter and Tate. "Johnny understands the Alaskan wilderness the way Darcy does. We grew up learning to shoot in case of trespassers or a rogue bear. Despite my carelessness a few days ago, we were taught how to spot signs of a potential avalanche. We learned how to use the wilderness to our advantage."

"Like firing at an overhang of snow and burying a team of police officers who thought they were well hidden?" Tate stared, assessing her like he was still trying to determine if the people who'd raised her were that in tune with their surroundings or she'd somehow given away their presence.

"Johnny was better than any of us," Alanna continued, ignoring the unspoken question—Tate was either going to have to trust her or she wasn't letting him in on her plan. "I can't have officers trying to surround him. Not with Elysia in the way."

Peter took her hand. "We'll be more careful about—"

"No." She turned toward him, Kensie's desperate face in her peripheral vision. "What I said before, about Johnny looking for revenge? I'm the one he thinks did him wrong."

"We're not going to let him hurt you," Colter hissed.

His loyalty brought tears to her eyes and she nodded a quick thanks to the brother-in-law who'd risked his life for her before he'd even known her to help Kensie bring her home. "I don't think he will. He's not trying to just lure me close enough to shoot me. He spent the past five years ignoring me. This is his way of reaching out."

Kensie let out a huffed breath, then leaned into her husband over Rebel.

Alanna kept her eyes locked on Peter, willing him to believe her, praying he'd have enough trust left with Tate to keep his partner quiet, too. "He wants to talk."

"Talk?" Peter asked, eyebrows raised. "And then what?"

"I know Johnny," she said instead of answering. "If we give him the opportunity to take me instead of Elysia, he'll jump at that deal."

"There's a better way than trying to make a trade," Peter insisted.

"Aren't we getting ahead of ourselves?" Tate asked. "Where is he keeping Elysia? Let's do some surveillance. We can—"

"You'll never get close to him," Alanna insisted. "But I can. I can go there and convince him to leave her behind. I just have to go with him."

"What?" Kensie stepped forward and Rebel did, too, giving a sharp bark in response to Kensie's distress. Kensie grabbed Alanna's arm, turning her so they were face-to-face. "I don't want to lose you again."

"You won't," Alanna said, forcing herself not to blink or shift her gaze. "He hates me right now, but I'm still his family. As long as I don't betray him by bringing the police, he'll go with me. He'll leave Elysia. I *know* he will."

"Alanna." Her name sounded like a sigh as Peter moved so he was in her line of sight, too. "You can't know how anyone from the Altier 'family' is going to respond anymore. Things have changed."

"You saw what happened in that cabin," she told Peter. "Darcy turned her weapon on you, but she ran instead of risking that she'd hit me. After everything that happened, Johnny is still her son. He'll do the same."

Kensie and Colter shared a worried glance and Peter's gaze lifted to Tate's, his forehead crinkled with doubt. Tate gave a short, hard nod and Alanna felt her whole body relax.

They believed her. They'd follow her plan. She let herself smile, because she knew it could work. Johnny had only grabbed Elysia to get back at her. He'd never hurt a baby. But no way did he want to raise one all alone.

"You can still go inside," Peter told Tate softly. "You don't know anything. You don't have to be a part of this."

Tate shook his head, the expression on his face a mix of anger and determination. "We've come this far because Alanna could predict what Darcy would do. If Johnny knows this place half as well as she does, he could disappear way too easily." His gaze darted to Kensie and Colter and then back to his partner. "Our department is good, but situations like this need one of two things—a good hostage negotiator or a full-time tactical team." He looked at Alanna. "I'll bet on our hostage negotiator."

"Thank you," she whispered. Then she took a deep breath and looked at her big sister. "He's at the cabin where we used to live. He must be. It's the only place he can be sure I'd know to look. I'll go up there and get in the car with him. We'll drive away and leave Elysia there. That way, he can be sure anyone coming after us will go into the cabin first. He's good at watching for tails. He'll see if anyone follows us."

"What happens if it doesn't work?" Peter demanded. "What happens if he tries to run with both of you?"

"I won't do it." Understanding that Johnny would probably be armed and there might be a situation where she had no choice, Alanna added, "If I have to get in the car with both of them, I'll signal you. Then you stop the car. Otherwise, you go in the cabin and get Elysia."

"What about you?" Kensie asked.

"Once we're far enough away, Johnny and I will talk things through. I doubt I'll be able to get him to turn himself in. But he'll know I won't stay with him forever, just like I didn't stay with the Altiers forever. He'll have to let me go."

They all stared back at her with worried expressions and she insisted, "I told you, he won't hurt me. He might take a while to let me go, true. Then he'll be a fugitive, because I can't bring him in if he doesn't want to go. But I'll be okay. I promise."

Chance whined, shoved his big head against her arm a few times, like he was begging her to be honest.

She stroked his fur and kept her expression even. Darcy would have been able to see through it, but the woman had raised her. Kensie had only known her for ten years, five of them as a little child and five as a woman torn between two worlds. But no longer. Today she was going to prove where she belonged.

If she didn't live through it, then at least she'd die looking after her niece the way Kensie had looked after her.

THIS WAS THEIR best shot.

Peter believed it, but he didn't like it. If this were any other case, he'd bring in his team. He'd trust them to do their jobs better than a group of civilians. Proceeding by the book would have meant officers surrounding the cabin, bringing in a state SWAT team if they had time. It meant keeping higher-ups abreast of every single movement of the operation. It meant Alanna would stay safely outside, far away from danger.

As much as he wanted that last part, Alanna was right. They wouldn't have captured Darcy without her. Darcy and her husband had taught Johnny how to shoot, how to hide, how to fight. Right now, sending Alanna into danger was their best shot at getting Elysia back to her parents safely.

Since Kensie and Colter hadn't immediately nixed Alanna's plan, they knew it was true, too. From the way they were staring at each other—fear, hope and helplessness all over their faces—they didn't like it any better than he did.

Of course, they didn't have to do it completely Alanna's way.

Her plan was probably going to save Elysia's life. But it was probably also going to destroy what was left of Peter's career. It would take down Tate with him.

Thinking about either of those things put a pain in Peter's chest, but Tate knew what he'd agreed to, understood what was at stake. If it meant giving Alanna the life she deserved with the people who loved her, the way it should have been all along, Peter could accept giving up what he'd only recently discovered was his life's calling.

What he wasn't willing to do was risk Alanna's life.

She could be right. She knew Johnny best, knew what he was capable of and, hopefully, where he'd draw the line. Whatever their sins, the Altier "family" had loved each other. But love that had turned into hate was dangerous. It was unpredictable.

They could trade Alanna for Elysia, make sure the infant was safe. But they needed a backup plan, needed something to trade Alanna for, too. Peter wasn't willing to risk Johnny driving off with her and having her disappear again from everyone who loved her.

Peter's family could really annoy him sometimes. His parents still treated him like a teenager. Their encounter with Alanna at the coffee shop hadn't been the first time they'd seen him around town with someone, assumed he was on a date and told the woman how badly he needed to settle down. His siblings weren't much better. They were all older than him, all happily married with kids and certain that what they had was all that was missing from Peter's life. That if he would only hurry up and find the right woman, settle down and make a couple of babies, he'd forget all about the reporter job he'd left behind, forget how hard he'd fought over the past year to be accepted at the Desparre PD as an equal, rather than a possible liability.

No matter how little he sometimes felt they understood him, they loved him. They supported him. And he'd gotten their support his entire life.

Alanna deserved the same thing. She deserved to

watch her niece grow up safe and happy and surrounded by her real family.

If he was being honest with himself, she made him see what his family was always insisting he needed. If she lived in Alaska, he could imagine dating her, could imagine one day marrying her and making babies, little miniature versions of her, maybe with his eyes.

It wasn't meant to be. But he wasn't going to let Johnny decide her future. Even if it couldn't be with him, Alanna deserved to have her own babies and watch them grow up safe and happy, too, surrounded by the family that had waited and searched for her for fourteen long years.

"I have a plan, too," he announced, making everyone's head swivel his way. Even Rebel and Chance looked up at him expectantly.

"Colter and Kensie, you should drive Alanna back to my place. Drop the dogs off there and wait for my call. Then Alanna should take her rental and you two should follow at a distance."

Chance and Rebel looked from him to Colter and Alanna, as if waiting for their reply. When there wasn't an immediate rebuttal, Chance barked and Rebel followed suit, like they didn't approve of the plan.

"Sorry," Peter told the dogs, as a smile broke free, the first one he'd felt since they'd gotten the call from Kensie. "But you two need to stay home this time." He looked at Tate. "I'm going to tell the chief that Alanna has good reason to suspect the baby is at the first cabin we went to, the one where Darcy started the avalanche.

I want you to go there with them, keep them looking. Keep them out of the way."

Tate shook his head. "I know what you're doing. You want to keep me out of trouble, hopefully save my career. But it doesn't matter. If you pursue this on your own and I looked the other way, it's the same thing as going with you. Face it. I'm in this. I'm with you."

"I want you to make sure the police go. I want you to make sure they're out of the way long enough for us to pull this off."

Tate crossed his arms over his chest. "Where exactly am I supposed to say *you* went?"

"Tell them I'm going to make sure Alanna and her sister don't try to get to Johnny first."

Tate shook his head. "You're trying to make things better for me and I appreciate it. But do you really think the chief will believe that I didn't know what was really happening? It would be better if I came with you. What if you need backup?"

"We'll be okay." He wasn't sure it was true, but this was about more than just doing whatever he could to salvage Tate's career. It was also about getting his partner out of the way. Because trying to take down a criminal without backup or following procedure was one thing. But what the rest of his plan entailed? Not even the closest partner would agree to it.

"I really don't think—"

"It's the best way," Peter insisted, knowing he needed to put this in motion fast before he thought better of it, too. He headed for the door, then pivoted back toward

Alanna, Kensie and Colter, who were all standing im-
mobile, like they hadn't absorbed his plan yet.

"Get moving," he told them. "Then wait at my place
until you get my call that the rest of the department
has cleared out. I want them far enough away that if
anyone calls them to a situation at the old Altier place,
they won't be able to respond quickly. But I also want
to do this now, while it's still dark. Hopefully give us
some element of surprise and keep Johnny off-balance."

His gut knotted at how badly this could all backfire
and he tried to ignore all his training, all his common
sense screaming this was a mistake. "Go," he insisted
again, and finally Colter and Kensie nodded, heading
for their trucks.

Rebel followed, but Alanna stayed where she was.
She shook her head mutely at him, studying him too
closely like she knew he wasn't telling her everything.

He wasn't going to give her time to figure it out.
Moving in close, he looped an arm around her waist,
pulled her to him and kissed her.

Her arms slid around his neck and she half leaned,
half fell into him as Chance gave a sharp bark. Then she
was kissing him back, the desperation in those kisses
telling him that what he'd planned was necessary.

She pulled back first, stared at him a long minute,
then spun and hurried to the truck where Kensie and
Colter waited. Chance barked at him once more, then
bolted after her.

"Let's do this," Peter told Tate, passing his partner
and reaching for the door to the station.

Tate put a hand on his arm. "What are you really planning?"

"Trust me, it's better if you don't know." He yanked open the door and went inside before Tate could argue.

Then he was running toward the chief, pasting a frantic look on his face that wasn't completely feigned.

She was on her feet and met him before he made it halfway there. They met in the middle of the bullpen, all eyes on them. Chief Hernandez looked from him to Tate. "What's happening?"

"Alanna and her sister and brother-in-law just took off," Tate said.

"I told them they could leave their dogs at my place and get some rest, then come back to the station. I said we'd call if we had any updates," Peter jumped in, not wanting Tate too involved in the lie. "I think they are going to drop the dogs off, but I don't think they plan to stay there."

The chief's eyes narrowed. "Why not?"

"I overheard Alanna telling Kensie and Colter that she thinks Johnny took Elysia to the cabin over in Luna, where Darcy started the avalanche."

"Why does she think that?" Chief Hernandez asked. "I saw the conversation between Darcy and Alanna. Darcy never said anything about that cabin."

"Alanna spent fourteen years with that woman," Peter said. "She can read between the lines better than we can. Look, she might be wrong. But do we want to risk it? We need to go out there. Actually…"

The chief's narrowed eyes shifted into a scowl. "Actually, what?"

"I should go to my place, see if I can keep them there, keep them out of the way. I might be able to get Alanna to listen."

"I'll go with the team," Tate said. "I don't know what Darcy said to Alanna, but she seemed convinced they'd be at that cabin. We need to go now."

Peter swore inwardly at Tate's addition, because it made him part of the lie, rather than someone who'd trusted the wrong partner. But Tate's word seemed to be enough, because suddenly Chief Hernandez was nodding and waving her arms for the rest of the officers to gear up.

As they raced to the equipment room to gather the heavier weapons and protective gear, Peter ran out to his SUV and whipped out of the lot in the direction of his house. Around the corner, he turned off his lights and parked. He slipped out of the vehicle and pressed himself against the corner of the grocery store, waiting until the last police vehicle raced out of the parking lot.

Then he made one quick phone call, before he ran back to the station. He used his key card to get in the rear entrance, knowing there'd be an officer who'd stayed behind. They couldn't leave the station totally empty, not with a prisoner in a cell at the back.

Hopefully, that officer wouldn't check on Darcy for a while.

Peter ignored the voice in his head screaming at him. Yes, he was about to break the law. Yes, it was against everything he believed in. But he couldn't think of any other way to ensure the woman he loved wasn't heading willingly toward her own death.

The woman he loved. The words rang in his head, ridiculous after such a short time knowing her, yet they felt all too real.

He'd worry about it later.

Slipping the cell keys from their drawer, Peter unlocked the only occupied cell inside the Desparre station.

Darcy stared at him, unmoving even as he yanked open the door.

"Let's go," Peter said, striding inside and pulling her to her feet.

She resisted, staring up at him suspiciously.

"You want *both* your son and daughter to still be alive by morning?" he demanded.

She stopped digging her feet in and allowed him to lead her as he whispered, "You're my backup plan."

Chapter Nineteen

A prisoner was handcuffed in the seat beside him; one he'd broken out of her cell. If his plan worked, she'd be back behind bars soon—and there was a decent chance he'd be headed there himself.

The whole thing sounded ridiculous, even in his head. When he'd first met Alanna, he'd seen her as his chance to finally find acceptance at the Desparre PD. Instead, he'd lied to the whole department and committed a crime inside his own station. How had this become his life?

Peter tried not to think too hard about the consequences as he maneuvered up the slick mountain roads toward a cabin well hidden in the woods that he'd only visited once before. Of course, his passenger knew the route from memory.

As soon as he'd gotten Darcy clear of the Desparre police station, he'd hustled her down the dark sidewalk around the corner to his truck, praying no shop owner was watching from behind darkened windows. Then he'd slapped handcuffs on her and pushed her into the passenger seat of his vehicle.

For a brief moment, he'd considered cutting Alanna out entirely, just driving Darcy up to the cabin and trying to make the trade directly for the baby. But he'd reconsidered before he'd reached the base of the mountain. It would be too hard to manage it all alone. The safest thing for Elysia was to get her completely away from the line of fire. At least with Alanna, she could walk toward him. How would he hold a baby while keeping his gun trained on Johnny? Even cuffed, there was no way to predict what Darcy might try. And while Johnny probably didn't actually want to raise the baby, Darcy might.

Besides, Alanna had asked him to trust her. Maybe she'd be able to get through to Johnny and end the whole thing peacefully. Maybe he'd even be able to slip Darcy back into her jail cell without anyone noticing she'd been gone.

Yeah, and maybe he'd still have a job come daylight.

Still, there was a chance. Somewhere on the road ahead of him, Kensie and Colter were driving up in one vehicle and Alanna in another. Alanna was supposed to text them all once she'd reached the cabin, then wait for their confirmation before she went to the door.

Once Alanna left with Johnny, he would follow. Kensie and Colter were going to get the baby and take her to safety. When he'd called to tell them to get moving, he'd gotten Colter off Speaker. The man had a leg injury he'd sustained as a marine that had never fully healed, but he still had a military mentality. If needed, Colter had promised to get his wife and child down the mountain, then come back up with a weapon and possibly Rebel. While her specialty had been tracking bomb-makers and she was long retired, she'd been military, too. Peter had worked with enough soldiers to know: once military, always military.

Peter hoped he wouldn't need them, but he did feel slight relief at the idea of having backup if everything went sideways. Overseas, the deadliest thing he'd carried had been a pen. But he'd been with soldiers, who'd been armed and ready to protect. Now on the force, he worked with a partner. But right at this moment, he'd never felt more alone. And it might be Alanna's life on the line.

"You're in love with my daughter, aren't you?"

It was the first time Darcy had spoken since she'd let him pull her silently out of the station and into his truck. She hadn't even protested when he'd handcuffed her.

He glanced briefly at her, remembering the harsh words she'd spoken to Alanna in the interrogation room. "If you still think of Alanna as your daughter, then you'll help me convince Johnny to let her go and take you instead."

"So, that's your plan. I figured it had something to do with my son. I didn't think you actually planned to let me go, though. You must really love her if you're willing to break the law. Or have you always been a crooked cop?"

He darted another glance at her, trying not to show how her words stung. Her opinion of him didn't really matter. But he did wonder what she thought of their chances of getting both Elysia and Alanna out of there safely.

She just stared back at him, a mix of curiosity, distrust and anticipation on her face.

If this went sideways, he'd have to worry about more than just going to jail. If he couldn't find a way to stop Darcy and Johnny after he got Alanna to safety, he'd be letting two child kidnappers go free. He had no doubts she and Johnny would start up right where they'd left off.

A ball of dread filled his stomach and twisted angrily. Peter clutched the wheel harder as the icy dirt roads beneath him became even more rough; this was an area that the town's snowplows didn't go. Anyone who lived up the mountain was tough. They lived at the mercy of the Alaskan wilderness and they always had a backup plan, too.

Peter darted one last glance at Darcy, hoping she'd be worth enough to Johnny that he'd give up his dreams of revenge. Hoping he didn't have his own plan that would leave all of them at his mercy.

The phone in his cup holder buzzed, startling Peter, and he glanced at it. *Alanna.* She'd arrived and was waiting for their go-ahead. Less than a minute later, Colter texted that he was in place, hidden off the side of the road. They were just waiting for Peter.

He hit the gas and his wheels spun out slightly. As he righted the vehicle, Darcy warned, "Don't drive us off the side of the road now. Not when we're so close."

She sounded too calm, like this had been her plan instead of his, and he tried not to let it worry him.

Then they were near the top of the mountain, still deep in the woods, as the first rays of morning sunrise started to filter through the trees. In theory, there weren't many routes off this mountain, just the main roads that snaked their way up and down, and they were sometimes impassable. But Alanna had lost him up here less than a week ago and if she could do it, so could Johnny.

He pulled the truck off the side of the road, far enough away that Johnny wouldn't be able to see him from the cabin. Then he took a deep breath and sent a group text. I'm here. Be careful.

I'm going in, Alanna responded.

From where he was positioned, Peter could see the very end of the Altiers driveway. He watched as Alanna's rental pulled in and then disappeared up toward the house. Now all he could do was wait.

Time seemed to stretch out forever and Peter couldn't stop his fingers from tapping a nervous beat against the steering wheel. Beside him, Darcy kept craning in her seat, trying to get a glimpse of the house. But it wouldn't happen. Alanna had told him exactly where to wait to stay out of view from the house.

Maybe he should go in. In theory, he'd be able to hear a gunshot from here, but a gun wasn't the only way to kill someone. Alanna was fairly tall for a woman and much stronger than her thin frame suggested, but he'd seen pictures of Johnny from five years ago. The man was six feet tall, even back then, and made up of all lean muscle. Plus, he was full of rage.

Peter glanced at the clock, then at his phone again. Ten minutes and no word. It was too long.

He was just reaching for the gear shift when an engine started up. The *clunk clunk* was familiar and Peter realized it was the same sound he'd heard at the last cabin. He mentally flashed back to that moment. Alanna had been getting through to Darcy. He'd seen the decision flash across her face, the recognition that it was time to stop running. Then that car had driven by—the old engine sounds grumbling—and she'd changed her mind. Johnny must have been driving up to get her.

Peter shook the memory clear as an old sedan backed down the drive. He grabbed the binoculars he'd stuck in his truck when he'd tracked Alanna on his day off and peered through them as the vehicle backed onto the street.

Johnny was in the car, but he was in the passenger seat. He glanced around, paranoia in his eyes but a smile on his face. He held a pistol, pointed toward the occupant of the driver's seat.

Peter glanced right and saw Alanna behind the wheel, her jaw clenched tight. As she stopped in the street, she gave an unmistakable triple nod of her head: the signal that Elysia had been left behind. Then the car shot forward, racing out of sight.

Peter held his breath as another vehicle pulled into the Altier cabin driveway. Peter backed into the street, then braced his foot on the brake, waiting.

"Come on, come on, come on," he muttered as Darcy demanded, "What are you doing? Follow them! Follow Johnny and Alanna! When I was caught, he ditched his phone to be safe. I don't have a way to get a hold of him anymore. Hurry!"

Every instinct he had demanded he pick his foot

up off the brake and stomp down on the gas, catch up to Johnny and Alanna before she drove right off the mountain and the two of them disappeared. But he'd promised.

"Come on!"

At his shout, Darcy jerked in her seat but went quiet.

Then his phone buzzed with a message from Colter. *We've got Elysia.*

Peter shifted into Drive and stomped on the gas, making the back of his vehicle fishtail as snow sprayed out behind him. Then he and Darcy were off, racing down the mountain, hoping to catch up to Johnny and Alanna.

THIS ANGRY, SNARLING man holding a gun to her head as she drove was the "brother" who'd once carried her half a mile through the snow when she'd twisted her ankle playing. The brother who'd wiped her tears away when he'd caught her crying over missing the family she'd been taken from. The brother who'd told her he couldn't wait to watch her dancing at his wedding.

Every time the old sedan hit a bump on the pot-holed road down the mountain, Alanna grimaced, hoping Johnny's finger wasn't on the trigger.

Her plan had worked. She'd walked up to the front door and Johnny had opened it before she could even knock. He'd held the gun on her, then glanced past her at the driveway. When she'd offered to go with him if he left Elysia behind, he'd scoffed. Then he'd stared at her a long moment, nodded his head and let her look in on a sleeping Elysia, content in an old crib.

"I know you're not here alone. They try to come for me and I'll take you out first, you got that, Alanna?" he'd asked.

The coldness in his tone had dried up her mouth and all she could do was nod.

"Then let's go," he'd said, ushering her out the door. "I don't need the baby. And I'd never hurt her anyway. But you and I have a score to settle."

That had been five minutes ago. Hopefully by now, Elysia was cradled in Kensie's arms, on her way back to her parents' cabin.

Since then, Johnny had just looked over at her and demanded, "Are the cops coming?"

Alanna had shaken her head and stared back at him, feeling truthful, because the only cop around was Peter. And he wasn't coming until Elysia was safe. Even then, he'd have to catch up to them.

Johnny had always been able to read her. Maybe because he was older or he'd known her for so long, he'd always been able to tell when she was lying. This time, he'd just smiled and ordered her to head down the primary road off the mountain.

"I never wanted to hurt you, Johnny," she whispered, the fear she felt coming through in her voice.

He snorted, not moving the pistol away from her head. "Well, you sure screwed that up."

She darted a glance at him, taking in the new lines just visible across his forehead and the harsh line of his jaw, now shaded with dark stubble, that had still looked boyish five years ago. At twenty-three, there'd been something sad and pensive if you looked close enough into his eyes, but he had usually worn a smile on his face. Now there was nothing but anger.

An ache filled her chest, knowing her note had ripped his life apart and he hadn't been able to put together a newer, better one. Sadness followed, regret that she hadn't tried a note years earlier, back before Darcy and Julian had asked Johnny to lure Sydney away from a playground. Back when it might have made a difference to the life of the older "brother" she'd adored for so long.

Was the person she loved even in there anymore? Or had all the good in him been warped and destroyed?

She swiped at the tears that suddenly blinded her and Johnny snapped, "You don't get to cry. You caused this. You caused all of this."

She shook her head, wishing she could pull the car over, that they could just talk like old times. "Johnny—"

"Didn't you love us at all?" he asked, his voice suddenly softer, more uncertain, like the boy she remembered.

The boy she'd hugged tight while he shook with suppressed tears after Sydney had first come to live with them, had cried and slapped him, telling him she hated him. The boy whose skinned knees she'd helped bandage after he'd fallen on the roof they'd been building, skidding halfway down the side before catching himself. The boy she'd tried to keep up with when he took her snowshoeing through the woods.

"I've never stopped loving you," Alanna said, letting her foot lift off the gas a little, slowing their dangerous speed down the treacherous road.

He snorted. "That's a lie." But he lowered the pistol slightly away from her head and there was less fury in his tone.

The Johnny she remembered was still in there somewhere.

Her heart rate picked up, hope sparking through the fear. "There's another way, Johnny." She spoke fast, not wanting him to cut her off. "It doesn't have to be like this. It should never have been like this. But I still love you. You're still my brother."

"And what about our mother? What about our *father*?" He lifted the pistol again and when she looked over, she saw the tears glistening in his eyes.

"I didn't want any of that. But you know what they did was wrong. What they made *you* do was wrong."

"They looked after us," Johnny said, but there was a tremor in his voice, as if he was trying to convince himself it was true.

She could get through to him. She just needed a little time.

Alanna lifted her foot a tiny bit more off the gas. She didn't know what the next stage in his plan was, but if she could stretch out this trip, where she had his undivided attention, then maybe she'd have enough time to get through to him. Convince him to put the gun down and turn himself in.

Her gaze darted to the rearview mirror and she pushed down on the gas again. She'd started out at dangerous speeds, speeds someone not familiar with the mountain roads probably wouldn't be able to match. But Peter was coming for her. She needed to stay far enough in front of him that she could talk Johnny down, but not so far that he'd lose her if she was wrong.

She loved Johnny. Despite the things he'd done, he'd been a victim once, too. He deserved the chance to rehabilitate, the chance to start a real life for himself. One that hadn't been built from lies, where he was surrounded by people who loved him without stipulations, who'd support him as he rebuilt something better for himself.

Still, if he refused to take this chance, she wasn't willing to give up her own life for him. She deserved a chance to really start over, too. She wanted to be fully honest with her parents, Kensie and Flynn, about how conflicted she'd felt for the past five years. She wanted the chance to travel to Kansas to see Sydney in person again. To talk to Drew's and Valerie's parents, explain that she didn't want to relive the past with their kids, but to build a future where they were still a part of her family, too.

And she deserved a chance to tell Peter how much he'd come to mean to her over the past week. If she survived this last drive with Johnny, she was heading home to Chicago. Three thousand five hundred miles was too far to build a romantic relationship. But it wasn't too far to build a friendship. It was less than she wanted, but it was better than losing him.

Before she could fight for Peter, she had to convince Johnny that everything he believed about Darcy and Julian was wrong, that everything he believed about her was wrong. She took a deep breath, then said, "They *did* look after us. But they stole from us, too. They stole our chance to grow up with other people who loved us."

He made another sound of disbelief, but it was quieter this time and the gun was lowering again.

"I met your parents, you know."

Back at the hospital in Luna, five years ago, Johnny's parents had shown up, tearful and excited to see their son again, just as she'd been ready to leave for Chicago. She'd shyly said hello and his mom had squeezed her arm and whispered, "Your parents are going to be overjoyed." Then she'd looked at her husband and added, "We couldn't even believe this was real."

"You did?" Johnny asked.

His gun was on his lap now, his expression a mix of suspicion and anger. But beneath it all, there was interest. Beneath it all, there was still hope.

Still a chance.

"Yes," Alanna said, her hand twitching to take his.

Then suddenly a truck flew out in front of her from a side road, making her slam on the brakes. Her head flew forward, the seat belt painful across her chest. The back end of the sedan fishtailed wildly, the vehicle not equipped to handle this kind of terrain. They continued to skid downward and she pushed the brake harder as the ABS activated, praying she wasn't about to crash into the vehicle stopped in front of her.

Peter's vehicle.

The car kept moving and Alanna heard herself scream, even though she didn't remember opening her mouth. Somehow the car finally stopped, with only a soft screech of metal as the front end scraped the side of Peter's truck.

Then everything seemed to happen at once. Peter scrambled out of his truck as Johnny's hand fisted in her coat, his other hand unhooking her belt. Then she was being pulled across the front seats, her body bumping every surface, surely creating bruises everywhere as she tried to help herself along. Suddenly she was outside the car, Johnny's hand still rough on her biceps, his pistol against the side of her head.

Across from her, Peter stood with his own hostage. Darcy's hands were cuffed in front of her, but the woman actually looked serene, a half smile on her face as Peter shouted, "I've got a trade for you, Johnny. Alanna for Darcy."

Chapter Twenty

Peter had destroyed his career trying to save her.

Alanna swallowed back tears as she stared at him standing behind Darcy, his gaze steady on Johnny, his finger resting above the trigger guard on his pistol.

The metal of the pistol barrel against her own head felt cold even in the ambient Alaskan temperatures. Johnny stood behind her, using her as a human shield, his grip painful on her upper arm, his angry breaths puffing against the top of her head.

She'd almost gotten through to him. But just like with Darcy, in the end, she hadn't been able to reach him. Not in time.

"Johnny—"

"Shut up," he snapped. Then louder, to Peter, he yelled, "What's to stop me from shooting you and taking them both?"

Alanna flinched, trying to twist in his grip despite the gun to her head. "No!"

"I'm a trained police officer," Peter said, his voice calm and steady. "You could miss and hit your mother. I won't miss."

She felt Johnny jerk at Peter's words, felt her own heart thud harder at the threat, at the idea of watching her older brother die right beside her.

"Your sister taught me something, Johnny. She taught me that love is stronger than hate. I know what you're feeling right now. You feel betrayed. You're angry with Alanna. But you still love her, just like she loves you."

"I don—" Johnny started.

"She doesn't want to go with you. She risked her life to protect her niece. You're her older brother. It's *your* job to protect *her*. It's your job to make sure she's happy. Let her go. You can take Darcy. The two of you can disappear. It's not right and you know it, but you can do it. Just let Alanna go. Please."

Johnny's hand loosened slightly on her arm and Alanna stared at Peter and the stoic determination on his face. It was probably all Johnny saw: a trained police officer who wasn't afraid, who'd be willing to shoot two kidnappers to save someone.

But she saw past that to the fear in his bright blue eyes. And she knew shooting Johnny would be his very last resort, something he'd only do if Johnny's finger started depressing the trigger on the gun to her head. She knew it was because she loved Johnny.

"Do it, Johnny," Darcy said. "Let Alanna go."

Alanna's gaze skipped to Darcy, saw the exhaustion on her face, the regret that said maybe she'd finally realized how many lives she'd hurt.

The hand squeezing her biceps released and the metal barrel against her head moved, redirecting to point toward Peter.

"Alanna, come here," Peter said, his gaze still entirely focused on Johnny as he let go of Darcy.

Alanna took a hesitant step forward, afraid any quick movement would startle someone, would make a nervous finger twitch against a trigger. Then she took another, her legs wobbly as Darcy moved past her in the other direction.

Darcy's gaze swung to her for the briefest moment, skimming over her face as if she was memorizing it. A sad smile flitted over her lips, then she mouthed something that might have been "Sorry."

Alanna took another step and then Peter's hand was on her arm, shoving her behind him as Darcy ran to the sedan and jumped in the driver's seat.

Johnny's gun stayed steady on Peter as he screamed, "Give me the key to the handcuffs!"

Peter tossed them over, his gun never moving off target.

Johnny caught them one-handed and jumped into the passenger seat. Then the sedan sputtered, the wheels spitting snow as Darcy, still handcuffed, maneuvered it around them.

Peter kept his weapon trained on Johnny and Johnny held his pistol in kind until the car was out of sight. Then Peter holstered his weapon and spun around, yanking her into his arms so hard she could barely breathe.

"I've got her," he said and it took her a moment to realize he'd pulled out his phone and was talking into it. After a short pause, he said, "Hurry. Darcy and Johnny are on their way down the mountain. They'll get off the main road now that I have Alanna, but we're close to the bottom. Come pick her up. I'm going after them."

As he hung up the phone and pulled back so he could look at her, Alanna asked, "How did you—"

"Darcy showed me a side road to get in front of Johnny's car. Colter and Kensie are only a few minutes behind us. They're coming to get you. I'm going after Johnny and Darcy. I've got to call in backup—I sent them all the way to Luna, but they might have figured out by now that it was a misdirect."

"Peter, you shouldn't have—"

"Don't worry. You're more important than a job."

Before she could reply, his lips crashed down onto hers. His kisses felt desperate, frantic, relieved.

She barely had time to wind her arms around his neck and kiss him back before he was pulling free. He smiled briefly at her, touched her cheek with his gloved hand and said, "I'll do what I can to bring them in safely."

Colter's truck raced up beside them and Peter jumped in his own vehicle. He waved a quick goodbye and then he was off.

Alanna stared after him until she couldn't see his truck anymore, then turned toward Colter and Kensie with tears in her eyes.

Was someone she loved still going to die today?

ALANNA WAS SAFE. But there were two kidnappers on the loose and it was Peter's fault.

The law said so, but so did Peter's conscience. He had a shot at catching up to them alone, at getting Darcy back behind bars before anyone at the station realized what had happened, but it was a long one. He'd be more likely to capture Darcy and Johnny with help.

He didn't call Tate as he maneuvered down the slippery mountain roads, scanning any bisecting road for signs of Johnny's car. He didn't want Tate implicated any more than he already was. Instead, Peter called Chief Hernandez directly.

"Where the hell are you?" the chief demanded, her voice a tight hiss. "And where is Darcy Altier?"

"You're back at the station?"

"Heading there right now. I got a call from Sam, who was stationed in the front."

"We have Elysia Hayes. She's safe. But Alanna traded herself for Elysia and I—"

"You traded Darcy for Alanna." There was no surprise in Chief Hernandez's voice, just a quiet fury that told him unquestionably that his career was unsalvageable.

The grief tightened his chest, made it hard to breathe, but he forced it to the back of his mind. "I'm almost at the bottom of the mountain on the Desparre side, trying to catch up to Darcy and Johnny. They're in an old mustard-colored sedan. Plates are muddied and unreadable, but you'll hear the car before you see it."

"You'd better hope like hell we find it," Chief Hernandez said. "For your sake and your partner's."

"Tate had nothing—" he started, but the chief hung up before he could finish.

Silently cursing Tate for jumping into the middle of his lie, even if it had helped sell it, Peter pushed his truck harder. Hopefully he wouldn't pass Johnny and Darcy right by as he hurried to the base of the mountain. Because once they got onto flat ground, they had more options, more ways to disappear. Darcy and Julian had stayed under the radar for eighteen years. Even once police had suspected she was in Desparre, even with her face so well-known from the media coverage, Darcy had still managed to avoid them. She'd probably still be at large if it weren't for Alanna. If Darcy and Johnny got off this mountain, he'd probably lose them forever.

Then he heard it. An old engine turning over and over, but not catching.

Peter hit the brakes hard, certain they'd heard him, too. He eased his truck slowly forward, inching toward the break in the forest ahead that suggested a side street.

Before he reached it, he stopped the truck. He left it running as he climbed out. Maybe it would give him a slight element of surprise if they thought he was still creeping forward in his vehicle instead of on foot. He texted a quick location to Chief Hernandez, then messaged Colter, too, telling him not to come any closer until help arrived. Then Peter slid his pistol from his holster, hoping Johnny didn't already have a bead on him through the dense trees.

He couldn't see the car yet and suddenly, he couldn't hear it anymore, either. They knew he was here.

Hurry up, he willed his team as he slid against the closest tree, moving cautiously forward. He couldn't wait for them, couldn't risk letting Johnny and Darcy get away again.

Johnny's voice rang out. "I'm a better shot than you give me credit for."

Peter froze, pressed harder against the tree as he scanned his surroundings. Could Johnny see him or was he hoping Peter would respond, give away his location?

"I'm afraid I'm going to need your truck," Johnny said as Peter twisted his head, trying to use his good ear to pinpoint the man's location. "Toss me the keys and I'll let *you* walk away. Otherwise, I'm going to have to take them off you."

He was straight ahead. Probably Darcy was too, although Peter couldn't rule out that she actually held the weapon. Johnny could be distracting him so Darcy could flank him and put a bullet in his head.

Except as Peter crept sideways, darting to the tree beside and slightly ahead of him, there was Johnny. He was scanning the forest, too, his attention mainly focused near Peter's still-running truck. Darcy was beside him, her hand on his arm.

As Peter lined the sight of his pistol on Johnny's center mass, Darcy's whisper carried through the woods. "It's over. You can't shoot him. Your sister loves him."

The weapon in his hands gave a violent shake before Peter righted it again, Darcy's words ringing in his ears. Why would she say that? Had Alanna said something to her when Peter hadn't been with her, made some calculated comment meant to help protect him that wasn't actually true? Or was it possible that Alanna was falling for him the way he was falling for her?

"We have to get out of here," Johnny whispered to her. "I'm not letting you go back to jail."

Darcy's hand pushed down on Johnny's arm, forcing his weapon to lower. "I don't want to go back, either. But I'm not letting you *kill* someone."

Johnny wrenched his arm free, lifting the weapon again, scanning the woods. But the expression on his face was conflicted.

Then sirens sounded, approaching quickly, and Johnny's pistol whipped in their direction.

If he fired at the police officers, they'd shoot back. Just like Peter, they were trained to shoot to kill.

This was Alanna's brother. And she still loved him.

Peter stepped out from behind the tree, keeping his weapon centered on Johnny. "Put it down. Please."

Johnny swiveled toward him, sighting his pistol on Peter's face, his gun hand shaking.

"Johnny, this is the moment that defines the rest of your life. If you fire that weapon, my team *has* to shoot you. Please don't make them tell Alanna you died here today. She loves you. She still wants a relationship with you. You still have a life ahead of you. *Please.*"

The sirens ended as the police vehicles came to hard stop. Officers jumped out, using the doors as shields.

"Hang on," Peter yelled. "Just wait! He's putting it down. Right, Johnny?"

Peter stepped forward and lowered his weapon, knowing the team had Johnny in their sights. "Please. Please."

"It's over, Johnny," Darcy whispered.

Johnny glanced at her, then lowered his arm and tossed his gun in the snow.

Then Peter's team was swarming the woods, pushing both Johnny and Darcy against the cars, frisking and cuffing them. Tate was with them, but he stayed back at the edge of the woods, his expression pained as he stared at Peter.

The fact that Tate was here right now meant at least his partner's job was safe. But his expression told Peter everything he needed to know about his own. He looked right and suddenly Chief Hernandez was beside him, hand out.

"Give me your weapon, Robak."

Even knowing it was coming, the request hurt. With shaking hands, Peter unholstered his gun and handed it to the chief. He didn't make her ask for his badge and just handed that over silently, too.

She gave a sharp nod over his shoulder and then Charlie Quinn was behind him, yanking his arms behind his back.

The sound of the handcuffs snapping over his wrists echoed in the woods and then Chief Hernandez shook her head. "You're under arrest, Peter."

Epilogue

Three weeks ago, when those handcuffs had closed over his wrists, Peter had felt the life he'd worked so hard for slipping out of his grasp forever. He'd glanced over at Tate through the trees, grateful that his friend wasn't facing the same treatment.

He'd spent a week in the Desparre jail. He'd asked his family not to come see him and told Tate not to let Alanna back to the cells, either. The last time she saw him wasn't going to be through the bars of a jail cell. At least that way, when she climbed aboard the airplane with Kensie and Colter, her last memory of him would be the kiss they'd shared.

He'd been sure his arrest would make the news. There'd be no way to hide it from her. But he hadn't wanted her to see him, to try to help. Hadn't wanted to give her one more thing to feel guilty over when it had been his decision. And he'd do it again. Even if it hadn't turned out okay in the end.

Now Peter handed over his ID at the tiny airport a few hours outside of Desparre. The next flight to Chicago left in two hours. Along with the three legs of the flight and the layovers in between, that meant he'd land in Chicago eighteen hours from now. Maybe in that time, he'd figure out exactly what he was going to say.

Alanna had called the station a few times over the past few weeks, trying to get through to him, presumably not knowing the outcome of his arrest, since the chief had actually kept it out of the press. Alanna had even managed to dig up Tate's number and had Colter call Chief Hernandez. He'd asked them all to just pass on that he would be fine, without giving any specifics. He didn't want to give her false hope, didn't want to open the lines of communication if he was going to spend the next five to ten years behind bars. Didn't want to say anything at all until he was one hundred percent sure.

Nodding his thanks to the clerk who handed back his card and took his luggage, Peter headed to security, which was light as usual. It was a small airport, mostly jumper flights in and out of Fairbanks.

After passing through the X-ray machine, he went straight for the big window to stare out at the vast snowy expanse that represented Alaska to him. He'd be back, of course. His whole family lived here. When he had told them about his plans, they'd all looked at him like he was out of his mind and then erupted with arguments. Until his mom had simply held up a hand to silence everyone. Staring straight at him, she'd asked, "Are you sure?" When he'd nodded, she'd smiled sadly and said, "I expect you back here every two months, minimum. Got it?"

With the promise secured, he'd headed home and

packed enough for a month. Hopefully in that time, he'd know.

Taking a deep breath, he turned his back on the openness of Alaska that he loved.

Then a loud bark made his head swivel and there was Chance, bounding toward him through the airport.

"What the—" Peter knelt down as Chance reached him and almost got knocked over for his trouble. "Easy, boy." He hugged the dog, looking over his head. "Where's Alanna?"

Then he spotted her, rounding the corner at a run, her rolling luggage making a *thunk thunk thunk* sound, her long dark hair trailing behind her.

He stood, running to meet her with Chance on his heels.

She skidded to a stop and he did, too, a foot away from her. Chance plowed in between them, walking through and back, punctuating each turn with a bark.

"Chance, relax," Alanna admonished, then stared up at Peter. "What are you doing here?"

"What are *you* doing here? Didn't you go home weeks ago?"

She settled her luggage next to her, slapped her hands on her hips. "Yes, when Colter and Kensie insisted there was no talking any sense into you, that you were never going to see me." Her eyes watered over, then she blinked the moisture away. "Why did you do that?"

He reached out, taking her hand. "I didn't know what my future held. I didn't want to tie you to it."

"I was already tied to it. It was my fault—"

"That's just it," he cut her off. "It wasn't your fault. And I don't want us to be connected by obligation."

She stared at him a long moment, then asked, "What happened? Last I heard, you'd been arrested."

"I was. But Tate talked the chief into filing things differently. *A police decision without proper documentation*, is I think how he framed it. That's not exactly how it ended up, but he saved me jail time."

Her shoulders relaxed, a smile lighting up her face. "So, your job is okay?"

"No." The smile faded and he squeezed her hand a little tighter, feeling awkward reaching across the space between them, but not willing to get any closer. Not yet. "I'll never be a police officer again."

This time, the tears did spill over. "Peter, I'm so sorry. I never—"

"Don't you dare apologize. It hurt, but it's not the first time I've left behind a job I loved. At least this time, it was a conscious decision. I knew what was on the line when I broke Darcy out. I got more than I deserved, because Tate is a damn good friend and Chief Hernandez can be nicer than she seems. And now…"

"Now what?"

He took a deep breath, suddenly nervous and very aware of how much he'd needed those eighteen hours to figure out what he was going to say to her. "I took a new job. It's a trial period, but I'm going back to reporting."

"Oh." Alanna's fingers twitched in his. "Back into a war zone?"

"No. I'm going to cover crime. With my background as a police officer and a reporter, they thought I'd be the perfect fit. It's not exactly where I thought I'd be right now, but I'm glad. I'm hoping you'll be happy about it, too."

"Well, yes. I'm sorry you can't be a cop anymore and I wish… Well, I'm glad you've found something else that excites you." She glanced down at their linked hands. "Peter, look, I came back here because I couldn't take all the silence. No matter what, I had to see you. I know we didn't have long together, but I…" She took a visible breath and Chance nudged up against her, as if to say, *Spit it out*, then sat at her side. "In the time we spent together, I've developed feelings for you. I want to see where that goes."

"Alanna—"

"Just hear me out." She stepped closer, almost close enough to kiss. "I know a cross-country relationship won't be easy. But I miss Alaska. I want to visit more. And I think you'd like Chicago. I really do. If we each travel to one another a few times a year, I really think—"

"Alanna, stop."

She looked at her feet, then back up at him. "I know you care for me, Peter. I—"

"I love you," he said, cutting her off. "I know it's fast. Too fast, maybe. But it's there and it's real and I'm not letting it go." He took a step closer, until he *could* kiss her if he just leaned down. "I'm not letting *you* go. I do want to travel back and forth a bit—my family insists on it, actually—but the job is in Chicago."

Her mouth dropped open and she just stared at him.

"I know you need to be there," he said softly. "It's

right that you should get time with the family you were denied for so long. You deserve that. And I want to be where you are."

She continued to stare until he let out a nervous laugh. "Too much? I know—"

Before he could finish the sentence, she was up on her tiptoes, falling against him, her arms around his neck and her lips on his.

When she finally pulled free, her cheeks flushed and her eyes sparkling, she whispered, "I love you, too, Peter."

Then Chance pushed his way in between them and Alanna laughed.

Peter took hold of her luggage and her hand, then spun back toward the entrance.

Alanna hurried to keep up. "Where are we going?"

"I'm thinking back to my place. I'm hanging on to it for when we visit here. What do you say we stay here for a few days, then head home to Chicago?"

She stopped abruptly, making him pause, too. "Home to Chicago." She smiled, grabbing hold of him for one more kiss. "I like the sound of that."

* * * * *

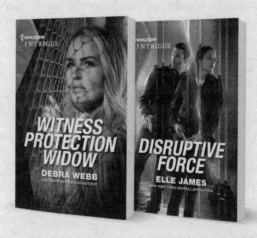

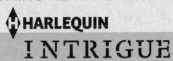

Prologue

The tears leaked out of Kay Duvall's eyes, even as she tried to focus on what she had to do. *Had* to do to bring Ben home safe.

She fumbled with her ID and punched in the code that would open the side door, usually only used for a guard taking a smoke break. It would be easy for the men behind her to escape from this side of the prison.

It went against everything she was supposed to do. Everything she considered right and good.

A quiet sob escaped her lips. They had her son. How could she not help them escape? Nothing mattered beyond her son's life.

"Would you stop already?" one of the prisoners muttered. He'd made her give him her gun, which he now jabbed into her back. "Crying isn't going to change anything. So just shut up."

She didn't care so much about her own life or if she'd be fired. She didn't care what happened to her as long as they let her son go. So she swallowed down the sobs and blinked out as many tears as she could, hoping to stem the tide of them.

She got the door open and slid out first—because the man holding the gun pushed it into her back until she moved forward.

They came through the door behind her, dressed in the clothes she'd stolen from the locker room and Lost and Found. Anything warm she could get her hands on to help them escape into the frigid February night.

Help them escape. Help three dangerous men escape prison. When she was supposed to keep them inside.

It didn't matter anymore. She just wanted them gone. If they were gone, they'd let her baby go. They had to let her baby go.

Kay forced her legs to move, one foot in front of the other, toward the gate she could unlock without setting off any alarms. She unlocked it, steadier this time if only because she kept thinking that once they were gone, she could get in contact with Ben.

She flung open the gate and gestured them out into the parking lot. "Stay out of the safety lights and no one should bug you."

"You better hope not," one of the men growled.

"The minute you sound that alarm, your kid is dead. You got it?" This one was the ringleader. The one who'd been in for murder. Who else would he kill out there in the world?

Guilt pooled in Kay's belly, but she had to ignore it. She had to live with it. Whatever guilt she felt would be survivable. Living without her son wouldn't be. Besides, she had to believe they'd be caught. They'd do something else terrible and be caught.

As long as her son was alive, she didn't care.

Don't miss
Hunting a Killer *by Nicole Helm,*
available February 2021 wherever
Harlequin Intrigue books and ebooks are sold.

Harlequin.com

Get 4 FREE REWARDS!

We'll send you 2 FREE Books plus 2 FREE Mystery Gifts.

Harlequin Intrigue books are action-packed stories that will keep you on the edge of your seat. Solve the crime and deliver justice at all costs.

FREE Value Over $20
